823.92 KIER

KU-942-609

Someone I never Knew

Thomas Kiernan

COPYRIGHT
2 5 OCT 2012
UCC LIBRARY

ABOUT THE AUTHOR

Thomas Kiernan was born in Granard, Co. Longford. He farmed for a few years after secondary school before going to live abroad. He has been writing for most of his adult life. He is married with two grown-up children and lives in Kilkenny.

This is his first collection of short stories.

Acknowledgements

I wish to thank Michael Massey for his friendship, his time, his help, his editing and his kind, constructive criticisms down the years. Also thanks to all of the Kilkenny Writers' Group.

I am grateful to Morgan Llywelyn for believing in me when I did not myself and for her help and friendship; to my friend, Ella O'Dwyer, for making this possible. To my friend, Leo Cooper, I say thank you for real-life inspiration and hospitality.

To Grace Wells I extend a warm thank you for giving me faith in what I was doing at a time when faith was in very short supply.

Thanks to Noel Monahan. To Pat O'Brien, many thanks. To my brother, Syl, thank you, and also to Shane. Thank you, to all my siblings.

Thanks to my late father and to my mother.

To my family, love and a great thank you, Alice, Tommy and Mairéad, my hardest and best teachers.

Dedication

for Alice, Tommy, Mairead
and my father

Contents

SOMEONE I NEVER KNEW

As soon as he comes in, I know something is wrong.

'Well,' I say.

'Oh,' he says. 'I had an accident.'

'A serious one?' I ask, though I guess it was. I see his eyes wander like he is looking for an escape. I turn off the dinner and sit. He is looking right at me now, a hangdog look that I fell in love with once. He stands there.

'Tell me,' I say.

'I was delivering, and scraped a car with the back of the truck.'

'And?' I say.

'I drove on.'

'You left the scene?'

'I suppose so.'

God, now the shagging thing is in the air. But I say nothing like this. I try to look calmly at him, but now he is looking out the kitchen window, out at those bloody old apple trees.

'Ok, let's have it,' I say. He raises his arms slightly, lets them fall again. He hasn't even taken his jacket off.

'I scraped a car. I think I did a lot of damage. Someone must have seen. The guards phoned me on the mobile an hour ago.'

Lord God! Now I feel like banging my head on the table, or banging his damn head on it. I do not.

'So, you left the scene of an accident.'

'I don't know. It all seems a blur.'

'What did you say to the guards?'

'Not much. I just said I was the driver of the truck and that I had been at where the accident took place at the time.'

'Nothing more?'

'I don't think so.'

'I hope so, Bill,' I say. 'This is serious and you're too old for this kind of thing. Come to think of it, so am I.'

He is staring at the floor again, probably wanting to disappear into it. If only he could. If only he bloody well could.

'Ok,' I say. 'Sit down. We need to get the story right. If you go in there confused like you are now, they'll work on that. Put words in your mouth. When do they want to see you?'

'Tomorrow morning.'

'We need to practise what you're going to say.'

'I'm going to tell the truth.'

'Of course, of course,' I say. 'Practise. Practise. We go through the whole story.'

He nods and we get on with it and I keep it up until the thing starts to get better. I throw in a few traps here and there. The first couple of times he falls in. I tell him, and we start again. Then again and again, until it comes out perfect. A perfect accident: no fault of his, he saw nothing, and he drove on. He's clear, innocent.

After he has eaten, showered and changed, he is composed, watching the TV, like everything's all right. And it will be, tomorrow, when he is interviewed by those guards. One of us turns off the TV at around half eleven and we are quiet for a good while, looking at the fire. He looks over at me after a bit, and he has a funny look on his face, a look I'd never seen before.

'I know you're strong, Marie,' he says. And I know I'd gone too far earlier on.

'I never imagined you like that,' he says then.

'Like what, Bill?' I say.

'Like a stranger. Like someone I never knew.'

And the way he looks at me, I know he means it.

I'll go with him

*T*he idea that he had killed her, slowly, drunkenly, dutifully, sometimes brought tears to his eyes, and he walked and walked with the sea to his left shimmering in the morning sun, his own shadow walking crookedly on the road before him. The backpack and tent were a drag on his shoulders, like the memory of her, and the old weight of her. He could not count the number of times he'd carried her like this back to the flat; lighter and lighter over time, as she tore into the habit, until it replaced her life's blood and she finally, towards the end, became light as an armful of straw, became the shadow impression she died in, and had left to him for keepsake, colourless, and foetal.

At a turn of the road, he saw it, the island, a few miles offshore, with the Dead Man island lying at its end, seeming to tell him all there needed to tell of the death of things and anyone's best efforts in life. He stood a moment watching across the water, the island green, brown and purple glinting softly in the light, and a small, white beach below what he imagined to be the ruined remains of a village. He would go over, bury everything there, if that could be possible. If he stayed long enough, it might be. He walked on then, until he reached the cove and he saw a falcon stationary in the air, high above the cliffs, before it swooped and he lost it from his sight. The ferryman remarked: 'A peregrine falcon. They nest in the cliffs, from what I understand.'

'I see,' he answered.

'You goin' over?'

'Yeah. Might camp there for a bit. That all right?'

'No law against it, to my thinkin'. An bhfuil an Gaelainne agat?'

'Beagán.'

'A start anyway.' The man laughed a short laugh to himself. 'We'll be leaving in a few minutes. I hope you'll be all right over there. You have a mobile?'

'Yeah. I'll be ok.'

'Take my number. You never know when storms set in. You get cut off over there

11

with no one to hear you but the wind and the sheep, maybe for two to three weeks at a time.'

'Thanks,' he said. He took the slip of paper from the ferryman. Then he stepped into the dingy and sat on the side, and waited to be taken over to the ferry.

He woke on the floor shivering, the whiskey taste in his mouth stinking with every one of his breaths. He propped himself up, and saw her across the room lying on her side with her knees up to the chin, a hand out from her, resting on the boards of the floor near to the syringe. He knew she was dead, and he stared a long time at her foetal form, the short, brown hair gone forward over the face, her red jumper and the jeans, and the thin ankles sticking out of the runners that he'd shoplifted for her, now seeming too big on her feet. He knew it had come at last to this, the end she'd been running towards for the past six months, deaf to him, blind to him, not giving a fuck for him, and she'd told him this repeatedly.

He pushed himself to his feet and shuffled to the door, pulled it open and stepped into the corridor. He made his way to the stairs, down then, to the street. It was daylight outside, and he blinked in the glare looking round him. He had to get away from here, walk until he could walk no further from a love that had become a nightmare. Old conversations spinning in his head, the lovely things she said to him before she got collapsed inward and the veins became hard to find.

He could smell the tang of urine along Talbot Street. He found himself in O' Connell Street. Early yet. What day was it? He needed something to drink, water, a mineral, anything. How much in his pockets? A tenner. Then for a second, he saw her again, a huddled-up shadow on the sidewalk, and he walked faster. She'd been born to take that shape, he imagined, reverting incrementally towards it, finally dying in it. He felt a distance rise softly in his chest, the sounds of the traffic on the thoroughfare becoming far-off, like everything was insubstantial, like he had not woken at all and that maybe if he closed his eyes he would wake up to something else, some other place, and he himself someone else.

Things needed to be done: a phone-call to the guards. There were rats and mice in the building. He could not leave her like that, unattended, friendless. Imprinted forever that foetal silhouette in his memory. He would remember her like that more than any other way, at rest finally, after a long swim through unimaginable places of ecstasy and horror: a broken universe.

He continued southward, over O'Connell Bridge. A shop attracted him in, something for his thirst, a carton of milk. He needed to be strong now. A job ahead. He would leave Dublin, but first this: a debt to be cleared, a slate cleaned. Then, a horizon of some kind. He stood outside the shop and downed the carton of milk, soothing in his mouth and guts. He began to feel strong. He set off again.

He knew well the block of flats where Mallory did his business, or at least some of it. He walked up the steps of the stairwell quickly as he could, ignoring the smells of dust and urine and the things under his feet that never failed to give him the impression that he was in a sewer of all kinds of hopelessness. On the fifth floor he walked out onto a corridor and found the door that was painted purple and he knocked three times and Mallory opened, standing there as always, like he'd just stepped in from a nightclub.

'It's you,' he said. 'Come for a deal?'

'Yeah, a deal.'

'How much you want?'

'Three fixes.'

'Not much. She on the methadone these times?'

'Yeah.'

'Come in.' Mallory led the way into the apartment. 'You got money?' he said.

'I've got enough.'

'I can always loan you a bit.'

'I'm all right.'

Mallory stood at the table, all business in his suit, his hair combed back, and designer stubble on his handsome face.

'You look shit,' he said. 'I've got a proposition.' Mallory sat down in a spell of old dust and human neglect that the apartment smelled of. On the table in front of him, a small travelling bag, a kitchen scales, a notebook and a pen.

'I see.'

'Same as before. You work for me. You'll have all the gear you need to keep her goin'. Plus a lifestyle you wouldn't believe.'

'I don't want to talk about this.'

'Listen. That's all. Just listen.'

'I'll listen.'

'See me? You think I live in this fuckin' dump? I don't. Course I fuckin' don't. I work outa here. And I have other places. Ok, I'm a fuckin' dealer. But I supply a product that some people need. If they die of it, it's because they've used it to excess. That's the way it is.' Mallory shrugged, made a gesture of futility. Then he said: 'I have so much money I have some of it stored in pillowcases. You think I'm joking? Work for me for one week.'

Mallory spread his hands; his features softened. 'You'll make a bag of money. Then see. I need a guy who's clean. I have a patch that's runnin', but I need a man I can trust to oversee it.'

'I'm still not interested.'

'Jesus. And all the robbbin' and wheelin' you do to keep her in gear. Plus all the money you earn in that crap job of yours. All goin' into that girl's veins. For how long? Two, three, four years. You know she's goin' to die or she's goin' to stop. Either way the choice is hers. Nothin' you do is goin' to change that. You can't save her.'

'I know.'

'Well, at least we agree on this. You should think about yourself. You've got prospects. I've heard of some of your stunts. Sellin' talcum powder to yuppies instead of coke. Fuckin' muggin' them sometimes. Work with me and you'd be on top. Also ..' Mallory spread his hands. 'You'd have lots to keep her goin'. Be serious and stop monkeyin' around. You'd be a millionaire inside eighteen months. I don't know

14

what to do with the money I've got. I've got cars, girls all over town.'

He threw a hand in the direction of the balcony. Through the glass door an opaque vista of concrete sprawl and development.

'She's dead. She over-dosed.'

Mallory stood up, walked across the room, pushed open the French doors to the balcony and stepped out. He cast his eyes northward across the rooftops of Dublin and the docklands to his right, the sea out there, barely visible in the haze. He turned facing into the room again.

'You came here to tell me this?'

'Yes.'

'I can't bring her back. Not now. Not last week. She was gone on drugs the time she left me. The only thing she cared about. Heroin.'

'She cared about you once.'

'She made her choice when she put the needle into her arm the first time. After that I lost out. What do you think I could do? Do what you did?'

'You were the supplier.'

'You have the balls to tell me that. You tryin' to make me responsible? Look to yourself. Look to your fuckin' self. When she was with me I gave it free. When she went to you, I charged for it. That's the way business works. Don't try to tell me I killed her. You were responsible as much as me.'

'She'd do anything for a fix. I had to keep her from whoring.'

'Well good for you.' Mallory turned his back and looked out at the city rooftops again. He brushed a hand through his hair.

'You came here to kill me,' he said.

'Yeah.'

'But you won't.'

'No.'

'Two reasons. I wouldn't let you, and your fucking conscience.' He tapped at the pistol that was stuck in the front waistband of his pants beneath the jacket.

'I think I'll go now.'

15

'Do that.'

He turned with the door half-open. 'What happened to us, Derek?' he said. 'Do you not remember the time when the three of us were together? School, soccer, the craic we had growin' up.'

'Course I remember. But I've moved on. You better go. I don't want to see your sad, fucking face again. Not ever.'

'I'm leaving Dublin. You won't see me again.'

He was mumbling to himself walking through Rathmines towards the canal, not knowing what he was at, the heat of the day enfolding him like a coverlet. His hangover had cleared. There were chores ahead, and preparations in the days to come for a journey that he would undertake. He had the feeling that wherever he went, it would have to be walked with his shadow before him, and that her foetal silhouette needed to be taken to some wild and peaceful resting place where seagulls, waves and wind could offer it endless comfort.

THE TWEED JACKET

He stood before her in the living room of their flat, wearing the tweed jacket that he'd been working on all the evenings of the previous month. He held his arms out from himself.

'What do you think?' he said.

'I like it very much, Anthony,' she said. 'It is perfect. You are really very clever.'

'Anna, this jacket needs an outing and this evening it will get it.'

'We go out?'

'A trad session. You and I will head out at approximately nine thirty. By ten we should be stepping in the door of Ryan's to the music of the legendary heroes of this land.'

'Heroes yes. Like you, Anthony. Together yes.'

'Together. And I will inaugurate the evening somewhere with a large Black Bushmills. Orangemen I know, but they make great whiskey, and for the occasion of my new jacket, nothing less than the best will do. On with us then towards Ryan's, the music and the craic.'

'The craic, yes. Anthony, this evening will be marvellous. And your jacket, I love it. You are the most intelligent tailor in Ireland and the most handsome.'

He took off the jacket and hung it on the back of a chair. 'I'm a lucky man, Anna, and you are the proof of it.'

She crossed the room and kissed him on the bristles of his close-cropped, red beard and as she stepped away he pinched her gently on the behind. She smiled round at him.

'I get some food ready. We do something Polish this evening. Perhaps we can allow ourselves a glass of wine in honour of your new jacket.'

'My love for you grows, my flower. Bring it on. I'll shower and change for dinner.'

He sat at the table eating, dressed in greenish slacks, brown shoes, white shirt with a pale, yellow tie and the brown, tweed jacket. She sat across from him. She had her black hair tied up behind her head and she was dressed in a blouse, black slacks and black shoes. She looked suitably regal, he thought. Perfect.

'This food is delicious. A recipe of your mother's I presume, Anna. My compliments to you both.'

She smiled at him and continued eating. When they had finished, she took a sip of her wine and said: 'I never thought being in love could be like this, Anthony. Now I understand how people could kill for it or go mad, even kill themselves for losing it. When you find love it is everything.'

He smiled. 'Anna, the man who tells you that he is a pacifist has never loved and probably never will. But maybe someone like you could change his mind.'

'This country is truly marvellous and so are you, Anthony.'

They were walking along High Street and couples and packs of young people passed them on the footpath.

'I've always been interested in clothes, Anna,' he said. 'I've always believed that if you want to know someone you don't need to talk to them. You just need to look at how they dress. There is always a statement there, especially with women. As for the men, Irish men, they seem to reflect in their mode of dress all that is wrong with us as a people.'

'I think you are being severe, Anthony.'

'They dress so carelessly. I firmly believe that they would be happy going around in animal skins. They dress so functionally and what their manner of dress says is: "Excuse me please. I have nothing to say that is worth saying." And when they bend over, without meaning to or even thinking about it they moon whoever is unfortunate enough to be behind them. A statement of a kind I suppose. I must grant them that.'

'Mooning, Anthony. I do not understand.'

'Something we copied from the Americans. I'll explain later.'

'Maybe we should go to Paris. Away from all this mooning.'

'No, Anna, my work is here. Anyway who needs Paris when I have you?'

She squeezed his arm and giggled.

'Now where will we have our primer?' he said. 'Cleere's, that's where. Soon I will have you introduced to the entire town, my lovely Anna. You know, I don't think I ever feared anything until I met you.'

'Don't tell me that, Anthony. You are without fear. It is I who am afraid.'

In the bar they stood at the counter and she drank a glass of wine and he a large Black Bushmills. His jacket was complimented on.

'Well, Tony,' someone said. 'Out in style this evening?'

'No bother, lads.'

'I have a suit that needs letting out, Tony,' another said.

'Bring it over any of the days. You know where I am.'

He drank carefully at his whiskey. She watched him, listened to his chat with the other men at the counter, and all the time while she sipped at her glass of wine, she kept a hand on his arm. The feel of the tweed cloth under her fingertips seemed exotic, magical, perfect. The cloth seemed to suggest an autumn that was only weeks away. She looked forward to the colours of that season, walking one of the roads outside of town arm in arm, kicking leaves before her boots. In the evenings they would light a fire in the flat. He would talk to her as he always did, and she would listen, savouring the words and the accent, so unlike the English that she had learned at school.

They had met six months before in Ryan's. He had been giving her the eye from his perch at the counter, and then he spoke to her, and finally he offered to buy her a drink. He had bought her a glass of wine, assuring her that pints would swell her out and that she was too pretty for that. She had smiled at this. He had the gift of making her smile, she realised.

They left Cleere's and went up the street to Ryan's and there too, there were complimentary remarks on the tweed jacket. They got their drinks and stood at the counter. The band was going full blast and already he was tapping his feet.

'Will you sing?' she asked him.

'If the banjo player gives me his machine I might,' he said.

During his third pint he left the counter and approached the band. The banjo player handed over his instrument and she listened to the song Sullivan's John. When he came back to her, she asked him about the song.

'It's about a man going off with the tinkers.'

'The tinkers. I don't understand.'

'Travellers, nomads, gypsies.'

'I see. But why do they travel?'

'Well there's a line of thought that says they were dispossessed of their land by the English. Personally I think they were driven off the land before that.'

'By who?'

'The Irish or maybe further back by the leprechauns.'

'I see. You will have to tell me something about these leprechauns.'

'You see pictures of them around Paddy's Day.'

'Ok but you will still have to explain to me. Perhaps later. There is so much about this country that I do not know.'

'I'm your humble servant, Anna.'

'This is a very strange country, Anthony. You know in Poland when people get drunk they become very stupid. Here when people get drunk they seem to become more intelligent.'

'Never realised that before,' he said.

After another two pints of Guinness, he had the tweed jacket draped over a barstool and he was dancing in front of the band. She watched. He took out different girls to dance and she had no fear until one girl stayed with him for a second tune. The girl was drunk, but she could dance well. Her skirt flew out from her legs as she twirled about in Anthony's arms and several times the edge of her white knickers became visible and she would give a loud whoop every now and again. At last he released the girl and came back to the counter.

'I've a fierce thirst on me,' he said, and he drained his pint to the bottom.

'You will have to teach me some of those Irish dances,' she said.

'I'm your man, Anna.'

'Does that mean that you will?'

'That's what it means. Tomorrow evening in the flat we will start with the basics. Jump two three, to some reels. I'll show you the moves and we do it together. In no time at all you'll be dancing in front of the band with me, driving the other lads mad with jealousy.'

'You know, Anthony, I was a little bit jealous while you were dancing.'

'There is no need, Anna. You are the only one for me and always will be.'

'I hope you do not drink too much.'

'Of course I won't, my dear.'

He ordered another drink and went to the toilet. She listened to the music. It seemed to go right through her limbs and made them want to shake in rhythm. She realised that even her head was keeping beat with the bodhrán. He came back from the toilet.

'Where's my jacket?' he said. 'My tweed jacket is gone. Anna, where's my jacket?'

'I don't know, Anthony.'

'You were here. Could you not keep an eye on it?'

'I don't understand.'

'Could you not watch it, Anna? Someone must have stolen it.'

'Don't be angry with me, Anthony. We will find it. I am sure.'

'We won't. A whole month of evenings went into the making of it and now it's gone.'

She was crying, her lovely face gone babyish and running with tears.

'I'm sorry. I'm sorry,' he said. He put his arms about her and rocked her until he could feel that she was calm again.

'It's only an auld jacket,' he said. 'I'll make another one. It's nothing to be upset over. I'm sorry, Anna. I get so foolish sometimes.' He stood back, smiled, saw her smile then.

They stayed until after midnight and went outside. They saw the drunken girl that he had danced twice with. She was sitting on the pavement with her back to the wall asleep, and she was wearing the tweed jacket. They stood looking at her for a moment. She looked comfortable lying there with her legs across the footpath and her arms folded, a dreamy smile on her features.

'I'd better not wake her,' he said.

'But your jacket, Anthony.'

'There's nothing valuable in it. She needs it at the moment. I'll leave it.'

'I'm getting that jacket, Anthony. Even if you no longer want it, I'm getting it back.'

She stepped forward and slid the girl's arms from the jacket; then she drew it upward from the girl's shoulders and folded it across her own arm.

'Now, Anthony, I have your jacket for you,' she said. She took his elbow and they walked on.

'You know, Anna, since you came into my life my need for you has been enormous. I'm eternally grateful to you for this.'

'I am grateful too, Anthony. Now should we get a taxi or should we walk?'

'A taxi. Definitely a taxi.'

RESPECT

I'm getting used to this place now: a hostel for homeless men. Guys like myself, separated from their past lives, cast-offs trying to make it back to normal living. We all have rooms. We can come and go as we like, as long as we check in before ten at night and have no smell of drink on us. Any whiff of alcohol and you are out on the street. You can come back the following day, and if you are drink-free, they let you in. The rules are simple, but strict.

In the good weather I go walking in the town, in the park, go into shops and sometimes a church. I have a curiosity that keeps me occupied. But I need to change the way I walk. It is a kind of drag in the step, a kind of putting as much time into the move as possible. You get to walk like this in prison if you are there for a while: a lag's step, Paul calls it. He'd been a guest of her majesty for a few years up North, he tells me. He had to relearn how to walk properly again. I've got to do it too. I'm out on early release, subject to good behaviour.

Barney is something else though. Sometimes I ask him if he ever considered politics. He's a class act at the bullshit. But even he can't get anywhere at the reception with the smell of drink on him. Sometimes I can hear the debate going on from my room. It starts off very civilised with Barney putting his case, denying the thing flat. What smell of drink? You're imagining it. Never touch the stuff. Must be that after-shave I put on this morning: Barney shovelling the shit and getting nowhere but deeper. The whole thing ends in a flying shower of fucks and the front door being slammed. Barney heading off to sleep rough somewhere. Dramas like this help to pass the time. Mostly I read. Paul plays the guitar. I hear him sometimes singing next door in his room. Some days I hear him crying. He's carrying his own share of horrors.

The sun is warm on my clothes and face as I walk in the park. The happy cries of children in the playground leave me peaceful and sad at the same time. I see a figure on the grass that looks like a man sleeping. I walk over, Barney fast asleep and his sports jacket draped over a shoulder. He is even snoring.

'Barney,' I say.

He stirs, looks up blinking those big innocent eyes of his.

'Matt,' he says, and smiles.

'You got locked out?'

'They smelled the drink on me last night.'

'Dole day. They'd be watching for that.'

'I need to get outa that place. It's like a fucking prison.'

'One you get locked out of, if you break the rules.'

'Very funny.'

He gets to his feet and brushes himself down.

'Fancy a breakfast?' he says.

'I've had mine,' I tell him.

'Have a coffee while I eat. C'mon.'

We go into a café and I sip at a coffee as Barney tucks into his plate of fry. 'I've a few ideas,' he tells me.

'You planning a breakout?' I say.

He gives me a severe look and then says: ' Look, I've been doing some serious thinking.'

'One of those darkest-before-the-dawn nights.'

'I have an idea for some work.'

'You have contacts?'

'I'll ignore that, Matt.'

Barney leaves his knife and fork on his plate and takes a long swallow of his coffee.

'C'mon,' he says then. 'As well as getting work, you might learn something.'

We walk out of the place and down the street and stop outside an auctioneer's office on High Street.

'On second thoughts,' Barney says to me. 'I think I better leave you out here. You're not respectable and you might say something that will blow the whole thing away. This is a charitable, Christian man who will help us if we approach him right.'

Barney goes into the building and comes out again ten minutes later with a smile of satisfaction on his face

'Go ok?' I ask him.

'Like a house on fire,' he says. 'You keep this under your hat for the time being.'

Two days later in the hostel there is a knock on my door. Barney steps into the small room and he's filling the place standing there. I push out a chair. He sits.

'Good news,' he says.

'Hey,' I say.

'Don't mock. Don't spit on lady luck.'

'Barney, I'm all humble.'.

'What were you jailed for anyway? Cynicism?'

'It doesn't matter, Barney.'

'Ok. So now is the new start. Never mind the other fellows in this place. They're all looking in the wrong direction. They're all fucked up. Paul there next door with his ballads about where have all the flowers gone and all that shit. That other alcoholic from Armagh who's in the process of putting the family farm down his neck. That big Dublin bollux who was inside for bouncing cheques, thinks he's descended from some fucking high king. They're all in fucking gaga-ville. You and me, we're different. Forget about those books that you read. I've got a few ideas. Follow me kiddo.'

'You know what happened to the last guy said that,' I say then.

'Very fucking funny, Matt. Just shut up and listen will you?'

'I'm all ears.'

'Here's the deal. The auctioneer has a row of houses that need

25

decorating. Twelve hundred apiece. You can do a house a week if you go hard.'

'You serious?'

'Deadly serious. I'm meeting the owner of the houses tomorrow, a respectable man. I'm going to draw up a list of things that we need. Paint, brushes, rollers, sandpaper, fillers, paint thinner, emulsion paint by the tub. You any idea how much paint it takes to do a house? A lot I tell you, a fucking lot.'

'How many houses?' I ask.

'Eight houses. Four each.'

I can't believe what I'm hearing. Four times twelve hundred is four thousand eight hundred. The idea hits me like a shot of whiskey. Enough money to go somewhere, start again.

Afterwards my head is in a fever. I walk in the gardens out back, down the town then and finally back to my room. I go to bed, but find it hard to sleep.

Two mornings later, I see Paul in the dining room at breakfast. I carry my tray across and sit down. He's all smiles.

'How's the songs going?' I say.

'Ok. Trying to write something. But it's blocked. Can't get the melody to work. I have a chorus, but that's all.'

'How's my walk comin' along?' I say.

'Not bad. Only noticeable to another lag. Probably it would fool your average, off-duty warder. Probably.'

'So I'm making progress.'

'You're making the right steps anyway.'

We laugh at this. He's a funny guy, Paul. When he's not the opposite: collapsed inward. I start to eat.

'I seen Barney,' Paul says. 'Must have a woman in his life. He's walking like a man who's getting a steady dose of great sex.'

'He's plotting,' I say. 'A new scheme, escape.'

'I hope he's not digging a tunnel.'

'His plans are in the early stages. I'll keep you informed as they go.'

'You should see him. He bought new clothes. Looks all snazzy.'

'He's on a mission and he wants me in on it.'

'You take care. Barney is one slick dude. He can even believe his own bullshit.'

'I've got nothing that he can take.'

'Don't forget you're out on early release.'

'I won't.'

Later that day, there is a knock on my door, and before I can say come in, Barney walks in.

'Thanks for knocking,' I say.

My sarcasm has no effect. He is on another plane, dressed in new slacks and leather jacket and shoes. He is wearing a Lacoste T shirt. I see what Paul meant.

'We have everything ready,' he says. 'You ok for some work?'

'Rarin' to go,' I say. 'Just point me in the direction.'

'Tomorrow after breakfast. Put on your worst clothes. I'll wait for you at the front gate at ten. That ok?'

'That's fine,' I tell him.

'We are on our way, Matt. Forget about your dole and earn decent money.'

'I'm your man, Barney.'

'You can buy more books for yourself. Get a flat somewhere. Able to go out, and pick up girls. Buy stuff. That's what respect's all about. Buying power, Matt. Buying power. Look at me.'

'I am looking at you, Barney,' I say. 'Difficult not to.'

Next morning I am up to my neck in work, sanding, wiping, brushing, and finally painting. Barney supervises me for an hour or two and gives me a crash course on getting rich. Some of the bullshit must be working because I am happy as I work, imagining all that respect coming my way. Buying power and girls and anything you want. Decent clothes anyway. The house I am doing will take me a week and then I can draw a cheque.

Barney has a mobile phone with Mr. Feehily's number on it. He is the owner of these houses. One bell from Barney and the guy comes running with a big, fat heap of lolly. Barney is working in a neighbouring house. That night I sleep like a man whose life is going somewhere good.

The next day I'm still hard at it. I have the bigger bedroom finished upstairs. There are two other smaller ones to do and a small bathroom, then the landing and the stairs, then the downstairs. I decide to leave the doors to last. With gloss paint they'll be tricky enough to do properly. The outside windows are priced differently. Front and back will be another four hundred. Around the middle of the morning I go out to the street and up to Barney's house. I tap on the front door and walk in. Barney in blue overalls is in one of the rooms sitting on the second step of a stepladder, smoking.

'Hey,' I say.

He looks up at me. 'Been doin' a bit of thinking,' he says.

'How's the work goin'?'

'Not as good as I'd like. Y'know with all the other things on my mind and having to run to the shop and buy stuff and taxi it up here.' He pauses a moment and then says: 'I'm all caught up in Mr. Feehily's plans. I need some kind of assistant. Thinking of getting one of the boys from below. What do you think?'

'Barney, don't. We have a good thing going here. A bit of time and effort and we'll be in clover.'

He looks at me like I'm raving, and I can see his problem: big patches of sweat on his clothes, and his face is dripping wet. He hasn't done this kind of work in years.

'A bit of time, Barney. Take it handy and keep going.'

'I promised Mr. Feehily. He'll be here on Tuesday. He'll need to see some progress.'

'My house will be ready.'

'You don't see the problem, Matt. You don't see it at all.'

I turn and walk out. I see the problem all right and I know exactly where all this is going.

The following day, the assistant appears. He is a tall thin guy from Dublin who who's been in and out of state accommodation since he was fourteen. Talk about a lag's step! He's premiership standard. Not a bad guy at all, but not part of our original plan. At the start he is the go-for: running up and down the street for the various errands that Barney has for him. By the afternoon,the guy, Ben, is painting Barney's house and Barney is doing the errands. I can see the progression of events. Barney as boss needs a team, and before two more days are out he has it: a whole flock of guys from the hostel and he's busy on his mobile, marshalling them about, giving them houses to paint, and keeping them supplied. By the end of the week some of the guys are sleeping in the houses. Matresses and chairs appear, radios and whatever home comforts can be pulled out of the town's rubbish skips. The houses are beginning to look lived in.

My house is coming along nicely, but then Barney appears with the guy from Armagh and wants me to share my house with him. No way José, and I use strong words to make my point. The guy, a big wreck of a fellow with red hair, just sits there on the bottom step of the stairs smoking, not even listening to what we're saying. An hour's work would kill him, never mind working up a ladder for days on end, and he'd be looking for his cut. He looks like he could do with a healer. I slip him a twenty and he heads off downtown: debate over. Barney leaves me, but I know that I've only bought time. Two or three days are all I need now. I'll have the house completed for the famous Mr. Feehily by Tuesday, take the cheque and run.

Of course my relations with Barney are getting strained. He arrives back with the Armagh fellow the following day. I slip the guy another twenty and he heads off downtown. I have bought another day. At this point I decide to bring in a few provisions and sleep in the place until it's finished. I do not sleep too good on the bare floor but that only means that I am up earlier. I go at the work like a madman: six in the morning until midnight, stopping only to eat, and keeping the doors locked against

Barney or anyone else who cares to knock.

On the Monday I am outside on a ladder painting the upstairs windows and the Armagh guy appears again. He gives the ladder a little shake to grab my attention. My position is vulnerable and he knows it. I go down the ladder and slip him a fifty this time after he tells me some old sob shit about heading up North to the funeral of some mate of his. That evening I am finished, but I tell Barney I am holding onto the key until the cheque from Mr Feehily appears. He glares at me when I say this.

'Eleven o'clock in the morning,' he says to me then. In his head he is probably calling me a selfish, capitalist bastard for turning traitor against the Alternative Republic of Barnovia. Fuck him, I say to myself.

I sleep like a baby that night on the bare floor and curled up in my sleeping bag. I am looking forward to getting back to the hostel and getting shaved, showered and changed into decent clothes. I probably smell like a Sumo wrestler's jockstrap, but life seems a bit better somehow, or at least it will be.

In the morning, at eleven on the dot, I go into our glorious leader's house. He has turned it into some kind of HQ with a table, chairs and notebooks, pens and documents scattered about. Mr Feehily is there, a small guy in a suit looking up a Barney. He is querying the signs of squat occupancy in his new houses and Barney is assuring him that overnight security is an extra service that he has thrown in to the deal, gratis. Some of the lads are standing around listening to this tidal wave of crap, finding it difficult to keep straight faces. They have been working hard too, but their houses are only half finished. They are enjoying the whole thing, in no hurry at all.

'I'm a simple man Mr. Feehily. I'm proud of this crew of mine. And we are proud to have you for boss. You have given us respect in our work. Your Christian principles are an inspiration to us all...................'

Barney goes into his childhood then, the hardships and honesty of those times that made him the man he is, and the lasting affection of his parents, Christian values, honesty, respect, etc. etc. etc. In the end I get my cheque and run from the place, straight to the bank.

I meet Barney on one of the corridors of the hostel a day or two later.

'You're baling out I heard,' he says.

'Time to move on,' I say. 'I'm enrolled in a computer course.'

'I could do with a bit of help down below,' he says then.

'Things not going well?' I say.

'Problems. That fucker from Armagh is looking for his cut.'

'Sure he did nothing at all.'

'I know. But he tells me the idea was his in the first place.'

'And was it?'

'Kind of.' Barney shrugs. 'His idea, but I got it going.'

'I thought he was gone North,' I say.

'He is. But he keeps phoning, looking for money.'

'Sure if he's up North, you're ok.'

'Belfast a couple of days ago. Newry yesterday.'

'Where's he today?' I say.

'Dundalk,' says Barney.

'Dublin tomorrow,' I can't help saying.

'He keeps getting closer,' Barney says. The thing is almost a joke, but I don't laugh. I can see the beads of sweat on Barney's face, the sadness in his eyes.

'I'll write you a cheque. Two weeks pay in advance. What do you say?' Barney says then.

I am nervous about chequebooks, especially one in Barney's hands. He has a car at this stage and things are generally rocking up at the houses from what I heard. The regime is shaky and I can't afford any involvement in the mess that I see coming.

'Sorry, Barney, can't,' I say. And he turns away with a look of disgust and disappointment on his face.

How do dreams die? They die hard. Always. I got the sequel a couple of weeks later from Paul. He even made up a song about it.

I was in the psychiatric wing of the local hospital visiting him. He'd had another bout of bad flashbacks and got himself committed. He was happy enough, getting the counselling and the care that he needed. I'd brought in a few books and filled him in on the latest news. He told me that Barney was in there too, just up the corridor. Did I want to see him?

I didn't, I told him. I'd had enough of getting rich the fast way.

DESTINATIONS NOT OF THE HEART

She saw him cross the street. He wore a jacket and jeans, and shoes that had never seen polish, just like the old days. But there was a drag in his step, something sciatic or maybe he was being careful of the patches of white frost on the road's surface. She fled into a shop.

'Twenty Rothmans,' she said.

'Have you started again, Máire? After all this time?' Mrs O'Hara said.

'No. They're for a friend.'

'Hardly anyone smoking now.'

'We're getting sense at last, Mrs O'Hara.'

'Well, whoever they're for doesn't have any. You tell them that from me.'

She paid and took the packet and shoved it into her coat pocket. She left the shop. No sign of him now. She turned up the street for her car. Her hand closed about the pack in her pocket and the memories seemed to come to some kind of life. Old, secret things from the early years: his car pulled in at the lake, the cuddling, kissing, and the talking and smoking until summer daybreak came up across the water and the fields. That was how it was: the daybreaks and the sleep-starved days at her work. He would drop her off at her house, she running up the pass, anxious to be in bed before her parents got up for the milking. A lifetime ago: the kisses, the face and the hands that she loved once. She got into her car and drove out the road towards home, finding a sense of old irritation coming back.

The careless gait of him, strolling across her memories, all those broken things. She could not blame him for the break-up, for she had thrown him out herself with hard words, and even when her blood cooled at the time and the sadness settled in, she knew in her heart that it could be no other way. He was of the type that would be held back in country places and local ways. He needed to experience elsewhere, go out foreign, do things with his life.

When she got home, she could not believe the sheer nerve of her sister who told her that she had met him earlier and had invited him to the house.

'I can't believe you did that,' she almost shouted.

'Lower your voice, Máire, will ye. Mammy's sleeping. How could I not at this time of year? He asked how you were, how Mammy was. Talked of Daddy. How could I not?'

She, her hand enfolded about the packet of cigarettes in her pocket, could only answer: 'I suppose you had to.'

'He didn't say that he would,' the sister said then.

All she could answer was: 'Well I suppose Mam will be glad to see him.'

Christmas came. They had their dinner under the holly and the decorations, she, her mother, her sister and her sister's teenage son, and it was a pleasant day of frost and sunshine outside. Neighbours called by and wished them the best of the season, and she detected the obligation that had brought them to the house. It was written on their faces as they sipped at their tea or their whiskey, and all commented on the severity of the weather and how the fringes of the lake nearby had frozen to a glassy whiteness about all of its circumference.

All those days she found herself anxious for his knock that must surely come. It did not come over the Christmas, and she thought that maybe he had gone off again back to his family or wherever he was living now. She had heard different stories of his present lifestyle. Most of them were hearsay and tinged with mystery, nothing that could be substantiated. Not until after the New Year, one Sunday morning, did he surprise her in her dressing gown, barefoot, and with a sleepy pallor on her complection. He stood there at the back door clutching at a festive present of some sort and said: 'How are you, Máire?' and held out his hand to be shaken. He kissed her swiftly on a cheekbone and waited to be invited in. She smiled at his

34

unease, feeling the weak, old urge to turn him away, and ignoring it.

He sat at one end of the kitchen range, his old spot, while she set the kettle to boil.

'You got me at my least best,' she said. 'We went to mass last night and lay in today. Great invention altogether, this Saturday evening mass.'

'Yes,' he said.

She sat down at the other side of the range from him, slippers on now, and crossed one knee over the other.

'I don't know what to say,' she said.

'Well, that's a start,' he answered.

'I was nervous about you calling. Nearly killed my sister over inviting you out.'

He nodded. 'Nothing to be nervous about. Just the past y'know.'

She looked away from him, across the kitchen towards the table and the back window. 'Nice of you to think of us. Mam will be delighted.'

'How is she?'

'She's good most of the days. Wanders a bit in her head.'

'We all do that sometimes.'

'Well, she's old now. Gets confused.'

'You're back here all the time?'

'Yeah, I'm back here. Family reared, husband gone.' She gave a small laugh. She could feel the scrutiny of his eyes, wondering how the same eyes had seen her pretty once, and he was in love with her.

'I'll wet the tea,' she said, getting to her feet. She looked at the present on the table. 'That for us?' she said.

'Of course,' he said. He smiled weakly, like he was apologetic. 'A few chocolates.'

She left a mug of tea on the range beside him and a small plate with some slices of Christmas cake on it. She sat and sipped at her own mug.

'Well,' she said. 'Just the two of us again in the old kitchen. Sister and lad out, Mam in bed, us alone here.'

'Old times, and us young. The walks along the lake,' he said.

'Young and not a jot of sense.'

'We were happy together.'

'We were,' she said. 'Course we were.'

'I heard you separated.'

'Why wouldn't you hear it?'

'Some things just go.'

'Some things.'

He was on her wavelength now, like in the old days, except there was no want anymore, no magic, just old, faded memories.

'It was no longer a marriage between us,' she said. 'So I left him.'

'Sometimes,' he said, and could not continue the sentence. He glanced at her once more, took a nibble at the cut of cake and sipped then at his tea.

'He could not understand anything that could not be counted up like two and two to make four. People don't work like that,' she said. She sipped at her tea, nodded then affirmatively.

'He never wanted to see anything that could be complicated. He was like a child afraid of the dark. We had big problems, and he had no interest in trying to solve them. No interest at all.'

'Therapy is good.'

'Oh, I did heaps of it. Yeah, it helped, and prayer.'

'I did a bit of therapy myself.'

'We were two of a kind, you and me. I always knew it, but no one else did. No one else.'

'Funny you say that. The obvious that we never said to each other.'

'My God, the way you talk sometimes. Years ago I thought for a while that I could put some sense into you.'

'I disappointed you. Sorry.'

'Go on ye auld chancer, ye auld charmer.' And she laughed for a long moment.

'Here,' she said, getting up. 'I'll bring Mammy down. She'll be delighted to see you.'

Later, she watched him cross the yard, get into his car and drive off, and he waved at her before disappearing at the gable of the house. She wondered would it be a further thirty years before she saw him or spoke to him again. She would be her mother's age by then if she was still alive, in all likelihood confused in old, misty memories of lakes, fields and distant kisses: the love that never went as far as it should have. She squeezed at the unopened packet of Rothmans in the pocket of her dressing gown and promised herself that she would walk to the lake and maybe drop off the cigarettes at the cottage of a neighbour, an old bachelor farmer who lived nearby; leave off that particular spell and stroll on. A walk by the lake, sometime before nightfall would ease the restlessness, calm things, before the memories dimmed to a point that would never hurt or enchant her with such resuscitated life ever again.

LAGAN LOVE

The house was sold and good riddance. Callaghan had been doing the rounds of the drinking dens on the nationalist side for the past week; he was insomniac now, almost sleepwalking. He reckoned he was in dire need of a shower; his bowels were loose and his bladder the same. He was paying his final respects to Belfast.

In recent months the killings were less numerous. The security forces seemed to be holding the nationalist rebellion to a slow simmer. There would be an upsurge close to Christmas. Halloween invited new efforts. It was the way it had gone for a long time now: seasonal tides of gunfire and bomb with the occasional, mutilated body being found on waste ground. He could go nowhere anymore without being ambushed by unease.

He had begun to feel the misappropriation of his life. In his work he was a watcher and a listener without any manifest powers of intervention. But in his head sometimes, things were seeping through the dyke: a cocktail of the smells from bomb-shredded intestines and cooked human flesh, and other variants of awfulness that he had sometimes believed he had become used to.

Still the reckless candour of killers from the various armed groups was something that mystified him. It seemed to him that despite themselves and their avowed deeds, in his presence they pleaded unconsciously some long-lost innocence. He had a notion it was this that drew him so easily into their confidences. He sometimes supposed they were beyond caring what they said because they were beyond caring for anything.

The Antrim Road with its autumn offerings of leaves left him nostalgic for his early days in this city before he had become blackened and all his mornings hung-over. He flagged down a passing taxi and jumped in beside the driver.

'The Shankill Road,' he said.

'Are you serious?' the driver said.

'I am.'

'I'm not goin' there. You want to get yourself killed you better walk.'

'I'll double the fare.'

'No way.' The taxi driver was shaking his head.

'I'll give you sixty pounds Sterling.'

'Are you fucking mad or something?' the taxi man said. 'Here give me the money. I'll take you. I must be mad myself.'

They drove off.

'I'm a journalist,' he told the driver.

'Are you a Catholic?'

'I was baptised one.'

'That accent. You English?'

'Irish, God help me. I spent my early years in England.'

'Maybe your accent'll save you over there. You goin' to interview people?'

'Kind of.'

'Three years since I was on the Shankill.'

'I can understand.'

'A friend of mine saw a dog cross the road there one time with a man's parts in his mouth.'

'You sure of that?'

'This man I believe. Haven't been over there since I heard that.'

All possible Callaghan thought. Bomb blasts send body parts flying. But then, there were rumours of a butcher gang over there. He resisted the urge to ask if the thing looked burnt.

'Terrible things taking place,' he said.

'Yeah. Lads being lifted and tortured. Disappearin'. No Catholic is safe these times.'

They were detained briefly at two military checkpoints and waved on. The taxi dropped him at the front door of the Cave Bar. A couple of goons in denim that he recognised were playing the poker machines near the door. He walked on by and headed straight for the toilets. While he was emptying his bladder and trying to hold his breath he got a push on the shoulder and one of the goons was standing beside him at the urinal.

'Callaghan,' the man said. 'What you doin' here?'

'I need to see Archie.'

'What about?'

'Private.'

'You and Archie get along pretty good together don't you?'

Callahan zipped up his fly and stepped back from the wall. He had a sense of danger, but it seemed distant somehow.

'Over here to do a drunk with ol' Archie eh?'

Callahan nodded. The goon's breath smelled awful. Had he been eating his dinners from the toilet bowl?

'Let me ask you something, Callaghan.'

'Go ahead.'

'How does this hit you? Me laughing into your screaming face and a blowtorch on your balls.'

'Given a choice between the two, I'd go for the blowtorch.'

The guy stared. It was clear that wit was a foreign language to him. Callaghan turned and went out into the bar. Too early for pints. At the counter a few barflies who ignored him. He ordered a large vodka and coke. The barman eyed him.

'Archie about?' Callaghan said.

'Over by the cigarette machine,' the barman answered.

Callaghan looked round. He saw the silhouette sitting at a table in a corner. The shadow waved over at him. He took his drink and walked across.

'Archie,' he said.

'How've you been?'

The brief flash of a smile from Archie. He motioned for Callaghan to sit beside him.

'Heard you were leavin' Belfast, Conor. We're gonna miss ye.'

'Thanks, Archie.'

'Why you goin'?'

'If I said that my life was in danger you'd probably split your sides laughing. I have a heap of reasons. Losing my job being one of them.'

'Well, the absent husbands on both sides of the divide will be easier in their minds with you gone.'

'Never realised I made such waves.'

'Conor, I saved your papish hide an unknown number of times.'

'Well thanks for that.'

'Och sure we couldn't have our boys killing a journalist. The reaction would be very negative.'

'The motive would be non-sectarian of course, a precedent for these times.'

'Not our line of business at all. I have to admit though that convincing some of our boys to leave you be, took a bit of doing. I told them, and I don't think I'm exaggerating, that you were doin' more damage to republican morale than you were to morale on the loyalist side. You had your pick I heard. Lots of boys in jail and their womenfolk needing comforting.'

'I'm glad my ecumenical efforts were appreciated.'

'Well, you'll be missed for that if nothing else.'

'I have to leave you know.'

'Every party has to end, I suppose.'

'My drinking has became a problem.'

'In Dublin it might be a problem. Up here it's an asset.'

'Dead right, Archie, but my body won't take much more. As for my head just don't ask.'

'Reason number two.'

'Yes.'

'I suppose you're goin' off to write a book about us. Make us all famous.'

'I don't think so.'

'Send us a card anyways.'

'I will. Will you have another?'

'I will.' Archie motioned to the barman.

'You have a new barman I see.'

'Yeah. We found that ol' Syd had been rattin' on us.'

'So he got fired.'

'In a manner of speaking yes. We had a chat with him about his contacts in the security services. Those bastards are supposed to be on our side. What do you think of that? Anyway, he filled us in some before we nutted him.'

'I'd not heard anything.'

'No. His body's not been found yet. The next day or so. Pity,' Archie said.

'I liked him,' Callaghan said.

'I suppose they got something on him and used that,' Archie said.

'Blackmail?'

'I think so, though he would not admit it. Said he was spying on us for money. But I always knew that Syd had no interest in women. What does that tell you?'

'The fatal flaw. Another reason why I'm leaving.'

'Reason number three.'

'Archie, every corpse I've reported on since my arrival here four years ago is a reason. I've viewed hundreds. I feel like a collector.'

'Reason number four.'

'No. Reason number two hundred and fifty four.'

'You've counted them?'

'Yes.'

'You've really got problems.'

'I know.'

'And you haven't even killed anyone.'

'You're getting the picture, Archie.'

'Listenin' to you makes a lot of other things seem ok.'

'I'm worn out with Belfast. Tired of always facing the door. I mean look at us, Archie. We're both facing the door. Those guys at the counter have their backs to it, but they're watching it in the mirror behind the bar.

Even in my house I have to sit facing the fucking door.'

'At least you've been gettin' paid for it.'

'Yes. But it's a horrible way to earn a living.'

'Write that book, Conor. Get it out of your system.' Archie put a cigarette in his mouth and lit it. He blew out the smoke.

'I've got reasons too for leaving,' he said. 'Fact is I've nowhere else. That's the trouble with us loyalists. We know we have nowhere else to go to. Nowhere we could be what we are.'

'If I'd said that to you, you'd probably shoot me.'

Archie looked down at the table and took a sip of his lager. 'Conor. I know well what I am: the guy who gets the dirty work done. Every armed conflict has guys like me. Without us loyalists, the British army here would be fighting blind. You know this. You've studied history.'

'Another reason for my leaving. I just can't help liking you despite what you do.'

'Jesus, you Catholics. I'd love to know the secret. I'm gettin' infected myself I think. Conor, I do believe I like your drunken, fornicating, papish hide.' Archie was silent a moment. He drank from his glass and took a drag on his cigarette.

'There was a couple we lifted sometime last year. The dirty work that I just mentioned. Gathering intelligence for our contacts that I'll tell you about later. It left an impression.'

'I don't think I want to hear this, Archie.'

'Conor, you'll hear it. I've something important for you. But first listen to this.' Archie took a drag of his cigarette and looked about him like he feared being overheard.

'This couple that we'd lifted from the Falls Road. The boy held himself well. Not a word from him even when Sammy over there broke the fingers of his left hand with a hammer, he didn't let out a sound from him so's not to frighten too much his girlfriend. We were looking for anything he might know, but he knew nothing. We'd heard of the wee girl's singing voice though, and Georgie asked her to sing.' Archie took a drag of his cigarette and kept his eyes on the smoke as it unfolded and swirled in front of his face.

'God knows I never knew it in him, that big ugly hunk of stupidity and the way she looked at him when he asked. And she sang My Lagan Love, smiling at us.'

'I knew that girl, Archie. I don't want to hear any more.'

'Where's the journalist in you? Are you not curious anymore, Conor?'

'Not anymore.'

'If there's a soul inside me I think the girl found it. I swear when that girl finished the last note of her song, none of us wanted to kill another Taig ever again. And that's why all of us fired shots into them both. We took them off and shot them while they stood holding hands on waste ground near the river.'

'I don't know what to say,' Callaghan said.

An interlude of terrible magnitude settled within him: a girl singing for her executioners. Shaking his head against the whole thing. He'd become accomplice, part of the chorus of bit players.

'Let's get another drink,' Archie said.

'She had black curly hair and freckles on her face. She was lovely,' Callaghan said. He was still shaking his head. 'I don't know why I can't feel anything. Why that is so. You shouldn't have told me this.'

'You're missing the point, Conor, and I'm in no position to lecture you. I'm getting a drink, a large vodka.'

'Yes, yes I'll have the same.'

'We'd not be talking like this without drink, Conor.'

'I've been drinking for a week steady.'

'I know something is wrong. When I was young I had that feelin', not knowin' what it was. Now I do know what it is: the kind of things that were never made known to us, and missing them. In prison I read a bit, and I'd hear the republicans singin' in their cells. Could never understand that in them. But now I think I can.'

'I've learned things too, Archie. But they keep me awake at nights, the things I've learned.'

'You're fitting in rightly so.'

'I've bitten into the forbidden apple.'

'Gone all biblical too. Stay here much longer you might pass for one of us.'

'I'm leaving this evening on the train to Dublin.'

'That's why I wanted to see you before ye go.'

'Right.'

'I've some things in the house you might be interested in seeing.'

'Photos?'

'Some photos, some files. A few things I wrote down.'

'Your contacts in the security services?'

'Yeah, the collusion that you always seemed so interested in. I'm being cut loose. I don't know how long I've got. A few days. A few weeks. I know a lot and that's why I'm a danger to my old contacts.' Archie drew on his cigarette and exhaled. He took a deep drink of his vodka.

'The wife knows what to do. She'll hand them over to you afterwards. It's your job to get this stuff into the papers.'

'At the moment I'm out of a job.'

'Do what you can. I'm asking you that.'

'I'll do what I can.'

'I'm not sure of anything anymore. I've done years of dirty work and now it's over. I needed to say what I said and you're the only person that I could say it to.'

'I understand, I think.'

Trying to get back again, Callaghan thought. What everyone wants when they find out things that destroy what they once were, always impossible to unbite the bitten apple. But Archie knew it did not matter anymore because he saw the end of the part that he had been born for.

Archie's face in shadow, a tired willingness seemed to glow from him. 'Maybe it was the girl singing that did it for me, Conor. None of us spoke of it afterwards. Maybe that's what did it, touched us in a strange way. Touched us, that girl singing.'

THE EXCURSION

Sergeant Flynn walked up the town one of the evenings in his uniform and knocked on Gallagher's door. Mrs. Gallagher answered.

'Sergeant,' she said.

'Is himself in, Mrs. Gallagher?'

'He is.'

'Can I come in?'

'Come on then.'

Gallagher sat at one end of the range in an old armchair with his feet out. He smiled. 'Come in, Sergeant,' he said.

Sergeant Flynn sat at the table. 'Sorry to be calling like this, Mickey,' he said.

'You're all right, Sergeant.'

Gallagher was dressed in a vest, pants and socks. His arms and chest were huge and his half-bald head was something that the sergeant could not take his eyes off: the scars across the scalp, engraved there with baton, fist and boot, an encrypted tapestry of battles fought.

'There's no chance of that money being paid, Mickey?' the sergeant said.

'Afraid not, Sergeant. Sure where would I get a thousand pounds?'

Sergeant Flynn took out a cigarette packet and offered it. He took one himself and lit for both of them.

'It's a hard duty for me, Mickey. Is there any chance maybe your uncle would come up with the cash?'

Gallagher shook his head. 'The auld General and meself haven't been seein' eye to eye lately,' he said.

'Would there be any point in me giving him a ring do you think?'

'No good. Sure the woman called. He told her I'd have to serve me

47

sentence. He told her that if it was in his time, he'd shoot me himself.'

'Ah Mickey, sure he hardly meant it. Sure blood's thicker than water.'

'Maybe so, Sergeant, but the General's thicker still.'

The sergeant rose from his chair. 'Your thirty days are up on Tuesday next, Mickey. Sure if the money's not paid by then we'll call around half twelve or one o'clock. That way you'd be in time for the evening meal. Would that suit you?'

'Ah sure I suppose it would.'

Sergeant Flynn held out his hand. 'I'm counting on you to take it easy with the lads,' he said. 'Don't give them any trouble, Mickey. Will you promise me that?'

Gallagher stood up and took the sergeant's hand. 'You needn't worry. Sure it was the whiskey done it to me. That, and the stroke of a baton from Guard Butler. That driv' me wild altogether.'

Sergeant Flynn sighed and walked out the door. On the street, he realised that the promise asked for had not been given. He walked off cursing to himself. By the time he reached the barracks he had started to sweat.

The obvious thing to do would be to pick four of his biggest guards. The trouble was, Gallagher might interpret that as bad faith, a challenge to be met. No, better be cute on this. He had a boxer from Roscommon, a young fellow called Malone. He could drive the squad car up. Then there was Doyle, who he knew to be an incorrigible porter-shark with his side-kick, Deegan, and there was an old hand, Cahill, who never issued a summons; he would be the diplomat of the team if the need arose. None of them were small men and they would have their batons, but the sergeant doubted they would be enough to stop Gallagher if he got going. It would take a machine gun to do it; that, or the old General himself. The whole business was delicate no matter how it was viewed.

On the Tuesday morning, he explained the plan to his team. 'Now don't forget, Gallagher's uncle is General Mulligan, former freedom fighter, former minister. Gallagher is probably the most important prisoner that you men will ever escort to prison in your entire careers. I know well what the man is like. But I know also that without whiskey, he's not a bad sort. I trust your discretion and your tact on this business. The evening meal in Mountjoy Prison is at six thirty. So have him in the gates around quarter to six at the latest.'

'That means if we leave the town here at twelve thirty, we have over five hours to reach Dublin. Sure all it takes it two,' said Doyle.

'I trust your judgement, gentlemen. Treat your prisoner well and keep him happy. You will be given an allowance for food and refreshment on the way.'

Doyle and Deegan nudged each other.

'Will it be all right to bring the prisoner in anywhere?' Doyle said.

'Treat the job as an excursion and make the prisoner part of the outing,' the sergeant said. 'Now if anyone is unhappy to do this I won't mind if you decline. If all goes well, you'll have a day out and be paid for it. If Gallagher gets difficult …' The sergeant spread his hands. 'You know what he did in the barracks in Mostrim.'

'Handcuffs, Sarge?' Malone said.

'Only as a last resort.'

'And if that happens, I'm sure he'll just hold out his hands and ask for them politely,' Doyle said.

Sergeant Flynn glared. 'You know what the man is like, Doyle. You've drank with him often enough. Now off with you. Keep all the receipts for me. And don't forget: the soft approach is the best one. Low-key all the way, got it?'

'Got it, Sarge,' Doyle said.

They got into the squad car and started up the street. Malone drove. 'I'm surprised the General didn't pay,' he said.

'He got him out of scrapes before. I suppose he feels that Mickey went too far this time,' Cahill said.

'I dunno if the Joy's tough enough for Mickey,' Doyle said. 'The fuckin' French Foreign Legion would be more in his league.'

'I've the feelin' we're on a suicide mission,' Malone said. 'We should be getting danger money for this.'

'And you a boxer,' Deegan said. They laughed.

'Sure we have the price of a few pints,' said Doyle. 'Handle Mickey softly and he'll be fine. I know he's all right on the pints. In fact I think that's the only way to go. We'll just coax him along. Make an excursion out of it like the auld sergeant says.'

'May as well. But keep him off the whiskey at all costs,' Cahill said.

Gallagher was standing by his front door, all cleaned up, shaved, and dressed in a short-sleeved shirt and new slacks and his shoes polished to a shine. He had a small overnight bag on the ground beside him. When he saw the squad car pull up, he stepped over. Doyle got out of the back seat and put Gallagher's bag in the boot. Gallagher got in the back seat and Doyle got in after him. Malone turned the car on the street and they drove out of town in the direction of Dublin.

'Well, Mickey,' Doyle said. 'How are ye?'

Gallagher shook his head. 'The woman was fierce upset. I tried to calm her. Told her I was headin' off with lads I knew but she only bawled more. It's a hard thing, headin' off to jail.'

'Only twelve months,' Cahill offered, turning his head from the front seat. 'The grub's all right and there's not a lot to do. You'll be fat as a fool coming out.'

'I know. Sure with good behaviour I could be out in six months or so.'

'There you are now, Mickey,' Doyle said.

Gallagher shook his head. 'She finds it hard all the same.'

'Women are like that,' Doyle said.

'I couldn't look at her the way she was cryin'. I had to lave the house.'

'You're with friends, Mickey. I hope you know that,' Cahill said.

'Indeed I do, lads.'

'And we might pull up for a pint in Castlepollard,' Doyle said.

'Ah sure that'd be grand altogether,' Gallagher said. 'I need something to raise me heart.'

'That's the plan now, Mickey,' Doyle said. He rubbed his hands together and slapped his knee. 'We'll pull in at the square,' he said. 'Mrs. Carroll pulls a lovely pint. Sure in weather like this you'd have to get it.'

They parked the squad car across from the pub, threw their caps into the boot and went inside; no one in the place but an elderly lady behind the counter. She looked startled for a moment to see the uniforms.

'It's all right, Mrs. Carroll,' Doyle said. 'We're only passing through.' He laughed.

'Five pints of porter,' Deegan said happily.

'Leave me out, lads,' Malone said. 'I'll have a couple later on.'

'All right, Ma'm. Four pints and a mineral for the gossun,' Deegan said.

The bar was shady and slightly cool, out of the heat of the day. The dust of the place swirled in sunlight that poured through the glass window, casting a spell of disordered ease across the barstools and the old boards of the floor. They had a second round of pints and Gallagher started to throw darts.

'Anyone for a game?' he said.

Malone stood in with him and they played down from two hundred. Malone won and Gallagher demanded a rematch. Malone agreed and this time Gallagher won on a bullseye. He slapped Malone on the shoulder. 'Ha ha,' he cheered.

'Leave it at that, lads,' Cahill said. 'A decent draw is no harm to either side.'

'Where are you fellows off to anyway?' the bar-lady asked them as they gathered themselves to go.

'A bit of an excursion,' Cahill said. 'That's all it is, Ma'm. A bit of an excursion.'

She pursed her features, guessing the errand on the traceries of Gallagher's head, but said nothing, even when Cahill asked her for a receipt for what they'd spent and to put it down as sandwiches and coffee.

They embarked and headed on as far as a roadside pub five miles further along. It was Doyle who prompted the stop and Malone obliged. They went inside and ordered pints from the bar owner.

'You fellows on business?' he enquired.

'Kind of,' Doyle said. 'A bit of an excursion.'

'Ah well,' the bar owner said then. He cast an eye over the uniformed crew, then at Gallagher, and he shook his head at some unspoken question. He served up their drinks, keeping a respectful distance from their company. Cahill started to peruse the racing pages of a daily paper that he'd found on the counter. They drank in silence. Finally, Cahill folded up his paper, downed his pint and said: 'We'll move along, lads.'

They drove through a countryside that was heavy in summer heat; haymaking was in progress. Gallagher shook his head periodically and kept silent.

'Who was the toughest man you ever fought, Mickey?' Doyle said.

'A tinker by the name of Mulvey at a horse-fair in Ballinasloe one time,' Gallagher said.

'Did you beat him?' Doyle said.

'No, but he didn't beat me either. We hammered away at each other for about fifteen minutes until in the end neither of us could keep going. We shook hands on it. He was a tough hoor. From Mayo, he was.'

'Was it for money?'

'Started off, he was starin' at me, so I stared back. He put fifty quid on the counter and said he'd fight me for it. We went outside to the yard and people put on bets. It was a good fight.'

'So if neither of you won, what happened to the fifty?'

'We drank it between us, that night and into the following day.'

'Jaysus, Mickey, you should have took to the ring.'

'Mebbe,' Gallagher said, and he shook his head again.

'We'll pull in beyond Trim and have a couple. I know a nice little place where we can get a feed,' Doyle said.

'And maybe a pint or two for dessert,' Deegan said.

'May as well, with the State paying for it,' Doyle said. 'What do you think, Mickey?'

'Might as well make the best of it I suppose,' Gallagher said. 'It's the last few pints I'll be havin' for a while.' He had his head down in the pose of a punished child, his two hands balled into fists and at his ears. The four guards glanced at each other; even Malone at the wheel managed the look of mute concern.

'Have an auld fag there, Mickey,' Cahill said. 'It's not the end of the world.'

'The woman,' Gallagher said. 'I'm gonna miss her somethin' fierce.'

'Why wouldn't you, Mickey?' Doyle said. 'Only natural a man'd miss his wife. Before you know it your sentence will be served. You'll have some good ones to tell us when you get back to the town again. You'll be fine. Sure, there's a couple of warders from about, up in the Joy. They'll see you right.'

Gallagher smoked and seemed to calm down a bit. 'Fuck the General anyway,' he muttered.

No one said anything. Cahill started to whistle an old ballad air. He let down the side window and rested an arm out to catch the breeze. Beyond Trim they ate a countryman's dinner at a wayside eating house and the four of them who were drinking washed it down with pints. Gallagher cheered up somewhat. The summer heat was intense, so they sat outside the pub on chairs in the shade of a fragrant hedge and drank and smoked and chatted until Cahill suggested that they should move on the road a bit further. They piled into the squad car. The talk became less cautious. Doyle asked Gallagher to recount details of the exploit that had led to his conviction for serious assault on three guards and extensive damage to a Garda station.

'I'm not sure what happened. It's like it was all through a mist. Soon as Butler's baton hit me it was like I was a living bomb.'

'So, what we heard in court was how it happened,' Deegan said.

'I think so,' Gallagher said. 'But I'm not sure.'

'Jaysus, Mickey, you could kill a man and not remember it,' Cahill said.

Gallagher nodded sadly. 'I just go wild,' he muttered.

University College Library Cork

'Tell us this, Mickey,' Malone said. 'Is there any man you'd fear fighting?'

Gallagher took a long drag on his cigarette and exhaled. 'The General,' he said. 'He's no youngster, but he's harder than rock. I couldn't bate him.'

They made two more stops and declared a final one at Clonee where they were near to the last of the expenses money.

'I think I should go on from here,' Gallagher said. 'I may as well face it.'

'Ah sure what's your hurry, Mickey?' Deegan said. Gallagher had downed his own pint in one long swallow.

'We've only started these ones,' Doyle protested.

'Sure I'll head on with young Malone here and you lads can hold on until he gets back from droppin' me off at the Joy. Sure it's only a half hour from here.'

'Mickey, you're the first man I ever met who was in a hurry to get to prison,' Doyle said.

'You lads finish those pints at your leisure. Myself and Guard Malone can head on in.'

'I don't mind,' Malone said. The four guards eyed each other. 'Why not?' Doyle said. 'Mickey is sound. Can we have your word on it then Mickey? That there'll be no trouble?'

'You have my word, lads.'

In the bar at first, they were stared at in discreet peeping glances, like their business in the place had been guessed at. The expenses money was gone so they drank from their own pockets in a quiet mode of satisfaction.

'Do you think he'll be ok with Malone?' Deegan said.

'I'm sure of it. Mickey has had his fill and he knows it. Beyond it he'd be at the tipping point,' Doyle said.

'He's fine without the whiskey,' Cahill said. 'Operation completed. When Malone returns we can beat it leisurely back towards home with a stop or two on the way.'

The bar-talk rose and fell in murmurous tides, the never-ending incantations of men whose days were tied up in profitless pursuits: horses, Gaelic football, women. They got drawn into it; their blue uniforms blended into the pub's sombre colours, character and chat. By the time Malone returned, they showed surprise at his state of sobriety and his refusal to have a pint or even a half-one so that he might more readily tune in to the wavelength.

'What's wrong?' Doyle demanded.

'I've got Mickey out there in the car,' Malone said.

'Don't tell me they turned him away. I know publicans do that when they see Mickey comin', but this is a bit much,' Cahill said.

'The General paid the thousand today. So we just bring Mickey back home,' Malone said.

'Jays, that's something,' Deegan said, shaking his head. 'The auld General lets Mickey sweat to the last and then steps in with the cash.'

'Bring Mickey in here,' Doyle said. 'Sure he must be lookin' to celebrate.'

'He's not,' Malone said. 'He had to phone the General at the reception. The old boy is going to have a word with Mickey next week.'

'The pound of flesh,' Cahill said.

'I never saw a man get sober as quick as Mickey after that phonecall,' Malone said. 'He's sober as a bishop out there and in a hurry to get back to the missus.'

'Oh well, here we go,' Deegan said. He drained his pint. 'We've done our duty. The next bit is up to the General.'

'Poor Mickey, Doyle said. 'The law works in mysterious ways.'

LOVE FOR LONELINESS

He'd arrived back empty handed. Couldn't be helped. He'd been lucky to get back at all. But he had no car and it was by pure chance that he'd met someone he knew on the ferry who had given him the lift from Dublin, dropped him off on the Main Street. He knew where to find Morrissey. Saturday night, eleven o'clock in the evening, where else would he be but in the Lucky Strike?

He walked into the public lounge and went straight to the counter and ordered himself a pint of Guinness. He could see Morrissey sitting in the corner next to the bandstand and he had a quare one with him, the two of them gaping up at the band. Typical of him, a new one every weekend. This new one was prettier than the others, and drunk as a whore by the looks of it, blonde and short skirted, legs that could haunt a man into old age. Suit Morrissey fine, give him something to yap about for a week or so. Morrissey waved.

He lifted his pint back in that direction, nodded, shook his head. He could see Morrissey frown then. In less that a second Morrissey was over to the counter.

'Well?' he said.

'Not well at all. I had to leave her.'

'Ye what?'

Morrissey's teeth were snapping at disappointing possibilities: a deal gone, and a waiting customer let down. His red hair came forward over his face. He brushed it back, propped himself at the counter.

'Tell me the story, Shamie. Tell me the fucking story.'

'The cops were at the quayside. No way I was goin' to drive that car towards the ferry.'

'Maybe they were watchin' for drugs.'

'They were lookin' at the cars. Any blue one that came along they were all over it.'

'Your one was blue?'

57

'It was. A blue Sierra. There was a blue Sierra queued up near the ramp and they pounced on it like dogs onto a hare.'

'So, you just drove away?'

'Not exactly. I was parked. I just walked down the line of cars that were waiting to board. A kind of scout around.'

'I don't fuckin' believe this.'

'You have to. I could be in custody this minute. This racket is all wound up. They're on to us.'

'I need time to think. What did you do with the car?'

'Parked it near the ferry.'

'If we go over and give it a bit of a change of appearance we could take it in by Fishguard to Rosslare.'

'You'll have to find someone else to do that.'

'Probably stolen by now.'

'Could be, who cares? It belongs to the rental company. All we lost was the rental and the deposit.'

'I lost that.'

'And I nearly got caught and my fingerprints are probably in it. Listen, Sean, an Irishman gettin' arrested for anything in England gets the full treatment and a jail sentence. You've lost money. I managed to get back here safe be the skin of me teeth.'

'We'll talk about this later. What'll ye have?'

'A large Hennessy.'

'A large Hennessy so.'

He felt like getting scuttered, ride off the release like that, get into some kind of party mood. He'd pulled his last stunt for Morrissey. Never again, not even if he was offered half the proceeds. The band was striking up another song, Tie a Yellow Ribbon round the Old Oak Tree. He gave a whoop and tossed back a mouthful of Guinness. Then he lifted the brandy and took a cautious sip.

The town was quiet further down where he lived, even the chip shop was closed. No one about. He breathed in the night air, savouring the familiar in it. He felt safe now. He'd come close to being nabbed. He'd used a false passport for renting out the car and kept his own in reserve. That's what had saved him.

He let himself into his building and went up the stairs. He was not too drunk but he knew he would wake with a hangover of some description. He felt ravenously hungry. He would cook up a fry straightaway, watch some late night film for a while, put on a video, old Clint maybe.

Lying back on the bed, finishing up his plate of fry, watching Clint Eastwood do in some baddies, heavy calibre bullets setting the world to rights the old fashioned way, half three in the morning and he falling asleep fully clothed. A knock on the door.

'Ye up there, Shamie?'

'I'm up. If I wasn't you'd have me up.'

'An emergency.'

'Never any other way. Always an emergency. Houl on there, don't break in the door.'

He put the video on pause and went over to the door and opened it. Morrissey and the quare one standing there. He stared at them.

'Can we come in?' Morrissey said.

He stepped aside and they walked past him and stood in the middle of the room. Clint Eastwood stared over the sights of his Magnum from the screen.

'Which one is this?' the girl said.

'Dirty Harry,' he said, shutting the door. 'Ye want a cup of tea?'

'Wouldn't mind,' Morrissey answered.

He made up some tea and poured it out for them and opened a packet of biscuits and spilled a dozen or so onto a plate and offered it. They were sitting at his little eating-table next to the window that gave to a backyard. He turned off the video then and sat on the edge of the bed behind them.

'You've a nice place here,' the girl said. 'Not like a man's flat at all.'

'You'd know,' Morrissey said. She was quiet then but the sting of anger was plain on her face and she sipped at her tea then like she hated the stuff.

'Spot of bother, Shamie,' Morrissey said, turning around.

The story of his life, trying to make the fast few pound, generally one side of the law, like the car racket he had going, renting a car in England, driving it over to Ireland and giving it a new identity, smuggling stuff, anything that promised a quick return. He worked up an expression that was close to a smile. It was the look that he used when he was on the point of selling a car to a doubtful customer, a kind of we're-in-this-together look, enjoy the ride.

'You better tell me, Sean. I know you're looking for a favour.'

'It's rubbin' off on ye, Shamie. Stick around and ye'll be as cute as meself before ye know it.'

'I'd have to stay a long time, Sean.'

'Hah, but yer gettin' good. For a fella that couldn't tell much about a car's inner parts three years ago to bein' a flyer at gearboxes and motors, sometimes I wonder which of us is the genius.'

'Pallaverin' me.'

'Theresa, would ye look at him? Me right hand man. Could I leave ye in safer hands?'

'You better tell me what it is ye want.'

Morrissey left down his cup of tea, put on a serious expression.

'Will ye keep Theresa till Monday morning?'

'Here? In this cubby hole?'

'Here.'

'Her father has fucked her out, damn near shot me when I pulled up at the house. I can't bring her home. Me mother'd have a fit.'

'Who's her father?'

'Buckley.'

'You afraid of him?'

'It's Theresa I'm thinkin' about.'

'There's not room to swing a cat in here.'

'She's off to Dublin Monday mornin'.'

'She a student?'

'Yeah.'

'I'm here too. Would you two fucking gentlemen please include me in this.'

'Right, Theresa, it's settled then. Ye have a bed over yer head and a roof under yer feet. Shamie here is the perfect gentleman. Not a hair of yer pretty little head will be molested in his care and yer honour will be safer than even in my own hands.'

He gave a laugh then and winked hugely, slapped one knee and rose to his feet.

'I suppose that means that I've agreed.'

'Yer not goin to refuse me after all we've been through, Shamie.'

He said nothing to that. Morrissey had answers to everything. He had the thing thought out at least an hour before.

'She can stay but where'll I stay?'

'There's room for two. Ye must have an auld sleepin' bag somewhere.'

All he could do was nod. When Morrissey left, they sat for a while without saying anything. He got up and pulled a sleeping bag from a press and threw it out across the floor.

'Is there a shower up here?' the girl said.

He explained where it was on the corridor and handed her a clean towel and a sponge with a bar of soap balanced on it. She kicked off her shoes and went out. He went over to the sink, threw some water on his face, brushed his teeth and put off the light. He took a pillow from the bed, threw it at the top of the sleeping bag. Then he stripped off to his underclothes, got in and zipped himself up.

She came in after a bit and he could hear her undressing in the dark and getting onto his bed. She said not a word and he, doubly aware of her uneaseful silence, dared not say a thing to disturb it.

He didn't mind too much the intrusion. He was tired enough to sleep on broken glass. It just felt a bit strange to be sleeping close to someone else's breathing, made him feel like a child again and for a brief moment brought on the old loneliness.

She slept soundly in the morning or at least pretended to. He got up as silently as he could manage, and in the half-dark, scarcely looking at the blond head on his pillow, he went out to the bathroom and came back showered, shaved and fully dressed and went out the door of his flat. He kept his steps light on the linoleum of the corridor and on the stairs, and he went out onto the street and turned left up the hill to first Mass. No rain, a bright autumn morning with a touch of frost playing on the skin of his freshly-shaven face. He sniffed deeply at the air. It was curing his hangover already.

She was up, sitting at the table and sipping at a coffee when he came back with the papers. He threw them onto the bed.

'Somethin' for ye to read,' he said.

'Thanks.'

'You long up?'

'Half an hour. I heard you go out.'

'Didn't mean to wake you.'

'That's all right. You've a tidy little flat.'

'I suppose. It's so small I have no choice but to keep it tidy.'

She smiled at him over her mug. 'I've been checking the fridge. I'd love a fry. Mind if I cook up one? You're included of course.'

'Fire away,' he said.

'Ok.'

She got up from the chair then and he sat at the table, amused to watch her cooking up a breakfast dressed in a miniskirt and a top that generously gave off the contours of her figure. This one had the power, stuff that Morrissey craved and that she could dole out as it pleased her.

'Where were you? Not that it's any of my business,' she said over her shoulder.

'I was at Mass.'

She laughed, put a hand on a hip and turned to him.

'I'm surprised at you. A big fellow like you.'

'I go …..,' he managed, unable to finish the sentence, and his unease made her laugh even more.

'You don't really believe all that Catholicism stuff.'

'I wouldn't be able to argue that one with you. Maybe it's just a habit.'

'That's what it is, a habit. Get yourself free, Shamie. You don't need those habits.'

'Well, maybe you're right. But maybe you're wrong too.'

'Shamie, I've thought about these things since I was twelve and came to a decision. Why don't you do a bit of thinking on it?'

'I'll try. Just keep an eye on those rashers or you'll burn them.'

She laughed then, threw back her head, and he watched amazed, and somewhat at a loss.

They read the papers after they'd eaten then, not saying much, and when he was finished, he rose to his feet and told her he was going out for a pint. He would have something for the dinner with him when he came back, he assured her.

He nursed his pint at the counter of the Lucky Strike. Some of the locals threw darts and more of them read Sunday papers back along the wall of the public bar. Buckley sat on his own near to the end of the counter, his face red from drinking, his head down as if pondering on something monumental. Finally he came over, put his pint back down.

'How're ye, Shamie?' he said. 'Will ye have a pint?'

He sounded cordial enough.

'I'm just havin' the one, Brian, thanks.'

'I won't insist. Have to respect a man's wishes.'

'Some other time maybe.'

'Some other time I mightn't be drinkin'.'

'We'll meet up sometime.'

Buckley sighed wearily then, ordered himself another Guinness and a half one.

'I'm at a turning point,' he said. 'This town's too fucking small.'

'For business?'

'For everything.'

'I like to go for walks, Brian.'

'I've seen you heading out the road sometimes. For a young fellow you've strange habits.'

'Ah just …..' He did not know how to continue. Anyway, Buckley's mind worked good at twisting things up. Better not say too much. The hoor was looking for an opening, looking for his daughter maybe, or someone to blame for the row between the two of them.

'There is just no room in this town for two garages. All we're doing is cutting each other's throats.'

'You'll have to talk to Sean about it.'

'Tell him I've a proposition. I need to see him.'

'I'll do that, Brian.'

'You could work for me tomorrow. Tell me what he pays you. I'll double it.'

'I'll think about it.'

'I know you and him are friends. In business friendship doesn't last too long, remember that.'

'Thanks, Brian. I'll think about it.' He finished his pint then, got up from his stool.

'I've to go to the butcher's before they close,' he said then, and he walked to the door finding the tension inside him easing with every step. He was sure Buckley knew the whereabouts of his daughter. He half expected to be grabbed from behind and slammed repeatedly against the wall face first until he either passed out or Buckley got tired.

When he got back to the flat he said: 'I was talking to your father in the Lucky Strike.'

'What did he say?'

'Business stuff. He offered me a job.'

'Just to get at Sean. Did he ask about me?'

'No,' he said, and after a moment: 'He's not a bad fellow.'

'He's a bastard. He threw my mother out. Now he's thrown me out.'

'I don't want to get into it.'

'This fucking town. They're all plotting against each other, scheming and gossiping, never saying things out straight.'

'I'm an outsider myself.'

'That's right, play safe.'

He could see her pretty face become ugly, something of her father in it as she spoke her bitter judgements.

'He's probably paying for your studies,' he said then.

'Don't remind me, please.'

She had her head down, propped on a hand at the table. 'It's a bad thing to hate your own father, but I do.'

'He's a stubborn man, you're probably stubborn too.'

'Daddy's girl,' she muttered, and gave a bitter laugh. When she lifted her pretty face and brushed the blond hair back from it, he could see tears there.

'Don't be sad,' he said. 'Here, I'll put on a Clint Eastwood video.'

She met his eyes, and for the first time since he'd spoke to her he saw a tenderness that lasted for a bare second. 'Sure,' she said. 'Put on a video.'

He was thinking of all the ways that the world could be put to rights if only life could be made simpler, if only people stopped a moment before they did the bad thing, if only the choices were easier, and the hours in days plentiful enough to contain what people really wanted: a small bit of happiness and enough to get by. The baddies always wanted more than their due; that was the problem. In the videos Clint could set things right with his fists and his pistols.

He was tempted to tell her what he really believed, but the words failed him, and anyway she was not his woman, and never would be. Never.

They watched all of Dirty Harry and then went on to the westerns and he gave a commentary of sorts, which she seemed to enjoy. She would laugh and throw in some comment of her own and they would discuss the unfolding of each scenario and its possible outcome.

In the middle of High Plains Drifter she said, 'He's always a wanderer, isn't he?'

'Yeah, a wanderer.'

'A guy from nowhere.'

'That's it.'

'Total freedom.'

He put the video on pause and waited for her to say more. Clint was smiling evilly at some baddie, his hand ready for the fast draw.

'You'll spend your life here,' she said.

'Maybe,' he answered.

'You really don't know, do you?'

'No.'

'Whether you will or you won't.'

'I've no plans. I draw my wages, put a few pound aside, drink a few pints at the weekend.'

'I'm kinda surprised Sean never made you a partner, you two being so close.'

'He has the money. I've got fuck all.'

She stared at him, knew she'd touched a nerve for the word fuck was pronounced awkwardly, like he was unused to saying it.

'I shouldn't have said that,' she said. 'I'm sorry.'

He did not answer. He picked up a newspaper and buried his face in it. She went over to the bed then and lay back with one hand across her eyes. After a little while he put down the newspaper, stood up and said: 'I'm goin' out for a walk.'

'Fine,' she said in a pained tone, and then added: 'I did apologise.'

'Yeah, I heard you say it. It's ok.'

He pulled on a coat and went out, left her there, glad to be on his own. He walked down the street, beyond Buckley's garage with its showroom and two new Toyotas in it, past Morrissey's small garage two hundred yards further on, then out beyond the town. There was a local club football match in progress in the pitch off the road, a small crowd shouting sporadic support. He walked on, passed the bungalows with their lawns out front and the glistening cars parked in driveways. Further on he slowed his steps, let his eye wander over the fields off the road. The land was empty of cattle, empty of sound too, just the occasional caw of a solitary crow. A typical autumn Sunday, he supposed. He no longer felt angry with the girl. What was the point anyway? She was spoilt, and headstrong as her father. Maybe she was right after all. He turned about.

A misty air of pre-twilight hung over the town on his way back. Smells of cooking from doorways and of smoke from chimneys. He knew the town well now after three years in it, knew by heart all its variants of scent, sound and light that changed imperceptibly with the passing seasons; it was a small place where his blow-in status was never unnoticed.

He could smell the cooking the minute he came in from the street. It led him like a thread up the stairs to his first-floor flat. He knew immediately that she was cooking up a dinner: the steak smell and onions with mushrooms thrown in and God knew what else she was concocting. She even had the radio going at a low volume, soft pop songs of some sort.

'Hi,' she said with great gaiety. She had one of his old shirts tied about her by the sleeves and was bent over her work at the cooker.

'Smells good,' he said, putting as much life into his shrivelled tones as he could manage.

'I'm no expert,' she said without turning.

'I dunno about that, Theresa,' he answered, saying her name carefully, the first time ever he'd used it he realised. 'Anything I can do to help?'

'It's just about ready. You could set the table.'

He found two sets of utensils in the drawer beneath the table and set them out. Then he poured water at the sink into two mugs and set them also on the table.

'Any candles?' she said over her shoulder smiling round at him.

'No,' he answered awkwardly.

'Jesus you're slow. I'm joking, Shamie. Joking.'

'Right, ok.' He tried a laugh. The effort failed him.

She served up the food then: two T-bone steaks with fried onions and mushrooms and creamed potatoes. He sat in and she sat at her place beside him.

'It's good,' he told her.

'It's basic enough. It was good of you to get the T-bone.'

'I always do on Sundays,' he said.

'I see,' she answered. She was smiling at something but he took no notice.

'I keep myself as well as I can,' he said then.

'I see,' she said once more.

He was back at his eating, head lowered to the plate, cutting his meat with care and chewing it with no haste at all: the silent moves and ceremony of a man used to eating alone. At last, she saw him finish his plate and leave his knife and fork together across its diameter. He looked round at her not unkindly.

'I never cook usually,' she said. 'Only at weekends for my father.'

'In Dublin what do you do?'

'I eat on the campus or go to take-aways.'

'Lots of them in Dublin?'

'They're everywhere.'

'Sometimes I get stuff from the chipshop if I'm workin' late. Too tired to cook.'

'Mostly you cook though,' she said.

'Yeah, better job altogether.'

'Of course.'

Talking to him was an effort, though she was trying to be nice. He was the unforgiving type, she supposed, calculated in his conversation, every word measured out like he understood the barriers of his life. But he thawed somewhat as she told him of her student life and her plans to qualify as a pharmacist. The whole thing was beyond his comprehension, but she rattled on anyway and a few times she saw him smile and pass a comment that displayed a warmth or a kindness towards her. He rose at some point and gathered up the plates and the knives and forks and washed them at the sink. Then he dried them and put them away while the kettle boiled. He made up two mugs of coffee then and said: 'Wanna watch another bit of Clint?'

'Why not?' she said, and she smiled at his easy tone.

He selected The Good, the Bad and the Ugly and they both sat back on the bed side by side, backs to the headrest and watched. Halfway through the video there was a knock on the door and Morrissey walked in. He was smiling, but he had an air of urgency about him. He pulled off the coat he was wearing and hung it on the back of a chair and sat down on it back to front and smiled over at them.

'The video any good?'

'Not bad,' she answered. 'Where were you?'

'Shiftin' a few tyres over the border. Debts don't sleep, Theresa. I have to be on the ball.'

She said nothing then, glared up at the TV like the video was not on pause.

'Anyone goin' to offer me a cup of tea?' Morrissey said then.

She got up from the bed and set the kettle to boil. 'Anyone else for tea?' she said.

'Make it up for Shamie, Theresa. Three mugs of tea there.'

He felt that Morrissey's arrival had broken something delicate, knew that Morrissey knew it too. Two children playing barefoot in warm mud. Looking over at his friend made him feel like he'd done a betrayal or something close to it. He rose from the bed and crossed the room.

'Leave me out there, Theresa. I'm heading out for a pint. Leave you two together for a bit.'

He pulled on his coat and went out before another word could be said. He was halfways down the corridor when Morrissey caught him up.

'Don't come back for about an hour,' he uttered in an urgent whisper. 'I'm horny as fuck.'

'All right, Sean,' he answered, turning away and racing for the stairs. On the street, night had come down and the air was sharp on his face and hands. He passed by the chip-shop just as Buckley emerged, all smiles and with two bags of chips gathered to his massive chest. He said: 'Come on,

Shamie, and we'll have that pint.'

'I dunno.'

'Come on. A Sunday evening and you look like a dog ate you up.'

'I dunno.'

'Come on t'fuck. Have a pint or two with me. Half the fuckers in this town won't talk to me and the other half can't understand me when we do talk. Come on I need some fuckin' company.'

They went into the Lucky Strike and sat up at the counter, no one else in the lounge. The barman came down from the bar side and Buckley ordered two pints of Guinness. When he'd finished eating his bags of chips he took a long slug of his pint.

'Just the job after a few chips,' he said.

'Or even the other way round.'

'The salt they say.'

'And the grease.'

'That too,' Buckley said, and he lifted his pint and took another long slug.

Buckley looked tired, his face all lined and yellow-looking. He seemed like a man washed up on some shore of loneliness and harsh reality, the suit that he wore all stained from takeaway spills and pint dribblings, and holed discreetly at the back here and there from cigarettes pressed close surreptitiously by some of the local character assassins: attempts on him while in his cups. Like he gave a fuck for any of their feeble efforts. He had other suits to meet the public in when he got off his skite: back in the garage showroom selling cars, a couple a week. Making money in a one-horse town; let any of them try it.

'You see that daughter of mine, Shamie?' he said.

'No.'

Buckley gave a snort of laughter. 'Like I'd expect you to say yes.'

'I didn't see her.'

'Would you tell if you did? Ah what the fuck. But I'll tell ye somethin', Shamie, me boy, the only reason I didn't shoot that fucker Morrissey last night was because I believe he's goin' to land in the same

70

mess that I got meself into with her mother.'

Buckley rubbed his hands together with the joy of the thing.

'Still, maybe I'll give the hoor a right batin' anyway. As a reconciliation I could visit him in hospital, bring in a few grapes, and offer him a partnership. What d'ye think?'

'He wouldn't be much use to you if you break him up.'

Buckley was thoughtful a moment, ran a hand across his features, looking away for a moment.

'True. I need to be careful. And Theresa will need him in some kind of working order.'

'There's that too.'

'I better do it without losin' me temper.' He pondered silently for several moments, imagined the satisfaction to come. It would need control and a measured amount of violence. He nodded to himself, smiled.

'She's studyin' pharmacy,' he muttered.

'I see.'

'Yeah.'

'Yeah, pharmacy.' Buckley stroked his stubble and ran a hand back through his hair.

'Y'know it might just be the makin' of that young hoor.'

'The batin'?'

'Aye, plus my daughter and the partnership.'

'You think he'll go for it?'

'I won't leave him a choice.' Buckley chuckled then.

'I know all about his rackets. His cars got in from England. The tyres and parts smuggled in over the border. If I wanted to play dirty I'd have the fucker in jail tomorrow. No, Shamie, me boy, I think I'll adopt him. Is there a better way to do him in?'

'I suppose not.'

'Shamie, me auld son, without realising it you have just become my accomplice. Work for me. I'll double what he pays you. I hear you're a great little mechanic.'

'I'll think about it.'

'Think seriously about it. Yel get nothing from Sean Morrissey but hardship. He'll be in with me before Theresa finishes her year. In two years time she'll be qualified and Morrissey will be my son-in-law. Get in now and speed up the process.'

'I'll have to think about it.'

The evening became something like a carousel spinning out of control: pints and more pints with whiskey thrown in here and there. Buckley talking out the sadness of his abandonment in this fuck of a town where a man couldn't break wind in private. He felt he was some kind of small-town King Lear: a variation on a theme, except that this time the old mad father would hold onto his only daughter, grab his son-in-law permanently by the balls and in this way stay on top of things. If there was comedy in this version, it would not be at his expense. Apologies to Shakespeare of course.

'Think seriously about it,' he repeated. 'I'll see ye right.'

He was unsure how he got away from Buckley, leaving him to his ravings and his plans. He staggered down the street, down as far as the garage and went in around the back and fumbled in the dark with a spare key that was left under a mat and let himself by a side door into the workshop. He clawed his way in the dark by the pale shapes of half-gutted cars, gearboxes and entire engines that his steps encountered, and at one point he became adversary to a pulley-chain that ensnared him in its coils for several moments before he cleared a passage to the side office. He went in, squeezed himself by boxes of garage miscellany, put on a light, and plugged in an electric bar heater. He sat into a swivel office chair then and resting his head on the desk in front of him he fell immediately asleep.

That was how Morrissey found him in the morning when he came in to open for business. He gave him a shake and woke him up. He lifted his head and blinked, got to his feet and shook himself.

'Is she gone?' he said.

'I put her on the early bus,' Morrissey answered. 'This minute she's in the lecture hall soakin' it all up.'

'Good. I'm goin' up to the flat for a bit of a lie down,' he said then. He went up the street to his flat and went to bed.

He left for Dublin the following week, leaving no explanation for his sudden departure. There were things that he just had to get away from no matter what it cost. He slept in his car for some weeks before he could afford lodgings and his situation could improve. Slowly, his circumstances got better and he became used to the city. After a year, a wedding invitation arrived for him at his place of work. For a day or two, he wondered how they'd found him, but that was all the thought he gave to it. The invitation went unanswered.

Some years later, when he himself had started up a business and had married and had small children, he was in Henry Street doing some Christmas shopping on his own and out of the crowd they appeared before him: his old side-kick, Morrissey and his wife, Theresa. Half bemused and full of surprise they shook hands and made awkward small talk for several moments, but no invitation was offered by any of them to go for a drink or a cup of tea together, and he felt that maybe it was better like this, that some things just could not be revisited without causing damage. He understood this much, but when, without giving heed to what he was at, he shook Morrissey's hand and then gave Theresa a small kiss onto her pretty cheek, and he smiled for a brief moment into her eyes for her to smile back. But she was either blind to his sudden show of old affection or was wilfully unkind, for she would not smile, just nodded blankly at him before he turned away and walked off down the street.

THE STUDENT AND THE PRINCESS

The sounds of Pretty Woman blared across the grounds outside. He imagined a record player on a windowsill in one of the senior rooms, the release-arm of the player to one side so that the single played from beginning to end incessantly. He loved the song, the five note bass string intro, suggestive of sexual intent; but it was getting to him. He'd heard it too much, entire days of it. He had shut all the windows of the empty dormitory. The song entered anyway: a soundtrack on his idleness and the sunny days at the back of the school.

He put down his book, Hard Times, the Leaving Cert novel. In his head he had entire chunks of it by heart. He was just reading to pass the time.

There was an exam in two days, English, the only subject he was good at. He reckoned it would be a kind of flourish after his poor efforts at the earlier ones. The possibility of university was gone; he knew that now, the fact that he'd failed: five years down the drain and the cost of it all, as his parents would remind him.

He got up from the bed, walked out of the dormitory. He went downstairs and then outside to stroll in the pitches. None of the gang was anywhere to be seen. They could be studying, but that was unlikely. They could be in the woods or down at the beach, maybe up on the roof. These days in the near-empty school there was no supervision, just Paddy spying on them from a sullen distance saying nothing. They were beyond his discipline now. They ignored him and his glaring. He stood in his Franciscan's habit like some kind of medieval inquisitor, and his intuitive eyes seemed to cast them all to certain perdition.

He knew he could do pretty much as he liked these times, smoke openly, as long as it was outside the building, anything but blow it into Paddy's face. He lit up near to the end of his round of the junior pitches and crossed back over the little bridge on the river and made his way up by the handball alleys towards the swimming pool and the running-track. For a hundred yards or so he was into the range of Pretty Woman, and then it receded to a distant irritant as he headed on.

Every square yard of this place had a memory for him, mostly bad ones: fights with stronger, older boys, getting caught at things by the priests. He'd become a hardened offender over the years. It often surprised him that he had not been expelled. He had not rebelled though, just gone and done his own thing, took his punishment as a matter of course.

He saw the northern kids far off beyond the running track. Probably, they were just coming up from the army base where they were lodged: refugees from a Belfast that burned on the news headlines most evenings. They saw him and waved. Then they ran towards him, five of them. He knew their names, could even predict pretty much what they would say, good kids with nothing to occupy them but roam through the countryside, which they did.

They'd recognised the renegade in him he supposed. Even though his parents had money, he was like them. They could sense it, his careless shrug and the long hair that he never combed: some kind of hero figure.

'I saw our house on the news,' one of them said. 'The army's camped on the front garden.'

One of the others contradicted. 'Not yer house atall. That wan's on the TV's different.'

'It's all burned. That's why it's different.'

They followed him along arguing amongst themselves as to the shape of a door on a burned-out house. The tallest of the kids reached to just over his elbow. He felt like a pied piper of some sort with a cigarette in his mouth instead of a flute. They were under trees now, walking a path by the school bounds where the air was heavy with the warm smells of vegetation: grass, ivy, chickenweed and wild garlic. If he had the inclination for it, he would be plotting what to say to his father in two days time, how to tell Megan that their Dublin plans for September would never realise, a prelude somehow to adult things. But it was like the final exam that would happen anyway for better or for worse, like the results that would arrive by post, inevitable stuff.

He left the northern kids and their strange chatter, wandered off, out by the back entrance and down the fields from the road in the direction of the beach.

He followed the track along the field where the runners went during the school year several times a week to train. In the old days, they were led by Paddy, his knees pounding up and down in his maroon tracksuit, his chest out and exhorting: 'Come on lads. You're younger and faster, but I'm harder.'

The memory brought a smile to his face. In his first term in first year he had gone with them for a few weeks, but discovered quickly enough that he was in deficit at this, always struggling, breathless at the back, Paddy ignoring him, only interested in the stronger runners, the ones with excellence ready-made etched across their chests. These ones were marked for great achievements. It had occurred to him then, that there were other things to do besides providing an embarrassment at cross-country. Besides, his head at that time was full of naked women, and keeping his imagination under control was a constant occupation that Gaelic football gave him a respite from before he took up smoking, and then the football too went down the drain. He was into books at that stage and had started to play the guitar.

The beach deserted from north to south, quiet except for the soft wash of the waves and the lonely screech of an occasional seagull. The scene dazzled the eye, cleared his head somehow: all blue and white, rolling as far as the Welsh coast just over the horizon. He walked with the shoreline to his right up as far as the headland where signs told that it was army property from here on. He turned back and took a boreen up from the beach that led by the entrance to the army base and he came out onto the Belfast-Dublin road.

He stood a moment by the Cock Tavern where he knew the soldiers drank and his presence was undesirable and considered the Fox's Arms across the road, quaint, whitewashed and thatched, and that a pint there might well be an attractive option.

Shady inside the Arms and cool. He walked over to the bar-counter and a tall black-haired girl came close. He knew her from the school, had seen her working in the kitchen at the end of the refectory. Sometimes she pushed a trolley along at mealtimes and gathered up plates and utensils from the ends of the tables, always intent on her work and never meeting the shameless eyes of the boys. He had not seen her before out of this context.

'Well?' she said.

'A pint of Guinness,' he said.

'Are you underage?'

'Not by much.'

'You look sixteen.'

'I'm doing the Leaving Cert. How could I be sixteen?'

'I could refuse you, you know.'

'I know but I'm asking you nicely.' He tried a smile.

She laughed at his boldness, then nodded to herself before going down the counter to pull the pint. He liked her laugh, liked looking at her in her jeans as she walked away. In the shade of the bar, her profile at the tap and lit by sunlight from a window seemed ageless and compelling.

'There,' she said when she put his pint before him. He lit up a cigarette and offered the pack towards her. She smiled, shook her head.

'I've seen you here before,' she said. 'You're a wild one.'

'I don't think so.'

'Oh you are. You are.'

He counted out the coins onto the counter and took a drink of his pint.

'I don't feel wild. I feel tired.'

'The exams,' she said then.

'Yeah. Just one to go. The day after tomorrow.'

'You'll be fine.'

'Did you do the Leaving?' he asked.

78

'Yeah, last year.'

'Any regrets?'

'That I did not work harder, yeah. Anyway I passed.'

'I'll be the same.'

'You might think it but we're not the same.' Her tone was soft, but he was lost for what to say now. It was like he owed her something.

'I'm off to England in a month to do nursing,' she said.

'Will you miss it here?'

'I suppose. But I can't stay.'

'Why can't you?'

'And be a skivvy all my life?'

'You shouldn't use that word.'

'I've been called it. Why shouldn't I use it?'

He was stuck again for what to say. He felt ashamed, accomplice to something that was beyond him.

'England's the only way out. The only way up for someone like me.'

He imagined her efforts at betterment that lay ahead, saw the determination in the steel of her pale eyes.

'You seem determined.'

'It's either that or stay stuck.'

'Yes.'

He drank at his pint and smoked the last on his cigarette, dropped the butt beside him and ground it out on the floor.

'What will you do?' she said.

'I don't know. My exams have all been poor.'

'Does it worry you?'

'A bit. My girl is in Dublin. She was hoping that I would be in uni next year and that we would be together.'

'You could still get a job there.'

'I could, maybe.'

Silence for a moment, then she said: 'I'll stand you a pint. Cheer you up.'

'I don't mind paying.'

'It's all right. Mrs Whelan is away. It's on the house.'

'Do you get many in here during the day?'

'The odd tourist, sometimes a soldier from the camp. Father Jude.' She smiled.

'He's on the batter these days.'

'Do you think I don't know? Mrs Whelan left instructions for me to refuse him, to call the guards if I had to. I haven't the heart. All I'm afraid of is that the priests will call down.'

'He taught me maths.'

'Bet he was good.'

'He was good. He used to be drunk in class sometimes, staggering. We'd find it funny. But only afterwards. In his class we were as good as gold.'

'I know. He looks severe. But inside he's an auld softie. The way he talks to me, like I was royalty or something. Young lady, and would you mind, and gracious me, and so on. I like him y'know.'

'Yeah. You've got him all right.'

Her eyes had an extra light in them as she talked, leaning onto the counter towards him. She had nice breasts too, he reckoned, like captive little pet animals under her white T shirt. She became aware of his lustful silence and stood back suddenly.

'Do you boys ever think of anything else?' she said.

'I have to admit that it's a struggle.'

'You're a bould yoke,' she said severely. A moment later she was laughing at the blush on his face, and it was as much as he could manage to take a drink of his pint without spilling the head onto the counter. He lit up another cigarette.

'Do you have a boyfriend?' he said.

'No. But it's none of your business.'

'Just talking.'

After a moment, she lowered her head somewhat and said: 'I had a boyfriend but he's gone to the army. What about yourself?'

'We've been steady for two years now.'

'Bet she's nice.'

'She is. All this year I used to skip into Dublin on Sundays and holidays to see her.' He gave a small laugh. 'I got caught before Easter. Lost my senior room. Got sent to a junior dormitory.'

'These things end,' he said then. We're both too young.'

'Sounds like she's special.'

He nodded as she said this.

'What's your name?' he said then.

'Siobhán.'

'I'm Martin,' he said.

Wobbly in his steps going up the road, hoping not to encounter Father Paddy on one of his routine patrols. For certain he would detect the signs of drink. He crossed the running track, walking along its forbidden surface with heedless steps and went over to the main building with the sounds of Pretty Woman playing at his back and went on into the refectory.

There were just five or six occupied tables near to the shuttered-off kitchens to cater for the eighty or so Leaving Cert boys. He took his plate from a trolley and sat at a table where the gang were. They were a motley crew of long-haired like-souls: copy-clones of the Beatles or the Rolling Stones. They would play guitars and read poetry, and for the past two years of boarding school would spend their free time lurking in quiet corners and the woods about the place, and even sometimes the beach on the pretext of going running. They would slag each other and fantasise about Dublin and the women there, and all the dope they would smoke, the bands they would join. They never stopped slagging. 'Here's the poet now boys. Stephen D himself. Where the fuck were you, Martin?'

'Went for a walk,' he told them. 'Couldn't stand Pretty Woman anymore. Y'know lads I wouldn't be surprised if Paddy himself was playing it to get his own back on us.'

There was a general murmur that it was a shit song and that Paddy was the high holiness of pricks.

He drank his tea and ate at his bread, beans, chips and rashers, parrying the general slagging with vicious cuts.

After the tea, they went out onto the roof carrying their guitars and, with Pretty Woman playing faintly behind them, did a medley of Beatles and Stones songs, but the music of the thing fell apart, fell into the usual slagging, and he walked off to a quiet corner next to the stairwell door away from the rest and did a couple of Bob Dylan songs in a soft undertone. He finished on an Everly's song, All I have to do is Dream, and it seemed to him enough of indulgent efforts at stardom, for when he looked up again he saw the gang mutely regarding him, and looks of high amusement on their faces.

'He's thinking of Maggie again,' Stoner said, and then he started into an effort at Maggie May.

He got up from the roof with his guitar and went down the stairs to his dormitory. He had seen the northern kids over across the front lawn of the school four storeys down. He would go off for a ramble with them, clear his head of bullshit.

They wandered about the front of the school across the golf course towards the main entrance all around the bounds of the place, the school farm and the road. The northern kids hopped about him. They knew he was leaving soon and said that they would miss him.

'When are you going back?' he asked them.

'Dunno,' they clamoured. From what he understood, their houses in Belfast were burned out or just not habitable anymore. It was not safe up there, though they missed the sound of gunfire. It was like in the films, they said.

The evening sun threw an orange glow across the front of the school, on the windows to the classrooms and the study halls and onto the old stonework of the adjoining castle. He scanned the battlements with a careful eye. Paddy often spied from up there with binoculars that were probably night vision. It was either that or the man had cat's eyes. Not that it mattered anymore. He wondered if Paddy would miss the chase over the summer months. Maybe he would use the time to train in preparation for September and a fresh campaign. The thought amused him: Paddy doing the rounds of an assault course, exhorting himself along. 'Come on, Father Paddy, they're faster but you're harder.' It brought a smile to his face.

'What're smilin' at?' the northern kids said.

'Just something about Father Paddy.'

'Tell us, tell us,' they insisted

He told them then of his imaginary picture of Paddy. The northern kids just looked up at him puzzled.

He left them soon after, shaking hands with each one, because he did not expect to see them again, and he told them this. He went back up to his dormitory.

Lying on his bed, he scanned the pages of Hard Times at random, then he did the same with Macbeth, thumbing across pages that he was sick of looking at, not even noticing that Pretty Woman had been turned off for the night. It continued to play in his head through visions of Scottish mist and murder by sword and dagger.

He sat at his breakfast in the refectory the following morning, the gang on every side of him and she came pushing a trolley by the table, handing out bowls of cereal and jugs of milk and gathering up the plates and utensils that had been used. By chance he met her eye, and she smiled in his direction, and he managed a small smile back. Her face darkened to a grim mask as she saw his wavering of recognition. She pushed the trolley on to the next table and kept her eyes to her work. The gang had noticed and he felt stripped bare in their amused scrutiny, his face turning all colours of red. He felt found out, and aware that he had been weak in the crucial moment.

Summer colours above his head, the sky with wisps of cloud, blue behind. He'd had hopes of becoming a pilot once, but that all went with his desire to study. Now the bill had arrived: losing direction, being weak.

He walked everywhere, keeping alone. Once, from a distance he saw the northern kids on the prowl. Heading for the woods, he supposed. He saw the gang far off in the senior pitches. They were smoking and kicking a ball about. Father Jude he spied going for the back gate with eager steps. The other Leaving Cert lads were nowhere to be seen: the sensible ones. They were studying in their rooms.

He passed along the beach. He had missed lunch. The sound of waves rushing in at his feet was all he wanted to hear. He came to the headland, and stood several moments looking about him before sitting down on a rock, and from there he watched out over the sea as it rolled forward, endlessly reaching at him.

He walked up the boreen by the entrance to the army camp and at the main road crossed over to the Fox's Arms. The usual dusk inside, and Father Jude with his head on a table asleep in a corner by the public phone, the girl standing behind the bar. She had been reading something on the counter as he came in, a paper or a magazine, by the light from the window. She lifted her head and offered him a blank stare.

'The student,' was what she said, and the words hit him worse than the hatred that flashed from her eyes.

'I want to say how sorry I am, Siobhán,' was all he could manage. What he felt at that moment seemed beyond him to describe, even if he had a year to do it.

'I let you down. Please believe me how sorry I am.'

She nodded sadly at him.

'This has been a bad day for me. Very bad, Siobhán.'

'It hasn't been a good one for me either. I've given earlier notice in the school. I was leaving anyway.'

He was still off balance, like he'd taken a blow hard to the head, but he met her eyes as best he could and repeated how sorry he was. She smiled sadly.

'You see how it is here. That's why I'm leaving. There's night school in England. They don't care who your father and mother are. You're not held back. If you work you can get on and be as good as the next. I'll be a nurse if it kills me.'

He saw now that she was strong where he was weak. It made him want to put an arm about her, to hold her close.

'Will you talk to me Siobhán?'

'That's my job, Martin. I'll talk to you.'

'Not like that. Like yesterday.'

'I'll try. You want a pint?'

'Yeah, a pint please.'

Strangeness now on her face: a peculiar interlude that he wondered at. She could be anyone she wanted. That's why she was leaving. She put his pint on the counter and he paid.

'Going home tomorrow,' he said.

'You'll be glad.'

'Yes.'

'Any plans?'

'No.'

'Did you learn anything at all?'

'I learned to fail. Got kinda good at it.'

'Seriously.'

He shook his head. 'I don't know. Learned to play the guitar and a few songs. I've read a lot of books.'

'You're a bit of a dreamer I think.'

'I can't deny it.'

She laughed, and he found himself laughing with her. She became easier in her manner, became tuned to what he was saying as his second pint of Guinness kicked in. He spoke about himself and his interests, and his hopes for the future, and she became engaged in his chat and told some of her own personal things. They were both seekers he told her, though different in plan. She had one and he had none. He needed some kind of starting point, he reckoned, and it came to him like a haunting what now remained to do: phone his girlfriend and let her know how things were. He took a handful of change from his pocket and checked through it.

'I need to make a phonecall,' he said.

'I'll switch the line over,' Siobhan said, and she went off through a doorway for a moment and told him to go ahead. He crossed the bar before he had time to ponder the thing too much and change his mind. He squeezed himself in behind the slumped figure of Father Jude at his table, and the operator put his call through. She answered.

'Martin,' she said, and he could hear her gasp of breath as she said his name. In less than a moment she was into her familiar line of chat. He had to stop it.

'I've been telling you rubbish, Megan. I won't be in Dublin in the autumn. I'll never make it to university, so we won't be together like we planned. I don't know what I'm going to become or where I'm going. I've done no study for years and that's why I'm breaking it off with you. Because I have to stop here and start again.'

'You sound drunk, Martin. Where are you? We can talk this over at the weekend.'

'Don't, Megan. I'll write a letter and explain. Don't come down.'

Father Jude was on his feet now, all shaking himself, fidgeting with the skullcap on his head and getting his coordinates together of time and place. 'You don't have to shout at the girl,' he said.

'Who's that, Martin?'

'Father Jude.'

'Where are you?'

'I'm in the Fox's Arms and Father Jude is here beside me. He's drunk.'

'I beg your pardon, young fellow. I'm not drunk. Take that back. How dare you?'

Father Jude making all kinds of indignant shapes and waving his hands before him like he would lash out as he often would in maths class.

'I'm sorry, Father Jude. Just trying to talk something over.'

'Well, you don't have to shout.'

'I'm not shouting.'

'I'm hanging up, Martin. See you.'

'Don't,' he said before the line went dead and he was holding the receiver in his hand and listening to Father Jude's protestations about manners and gentlemanly behaviour, and how to treat young ladies.

'I'll never understand you young people,' he said and he slumped once more onto his seat, tossed back his Hennessy and ordered another.

'I don't know, Father, if one more would suit you.'

'Siobhán, do I ever cause you trouble or treat you any less than the perfect little princess which you indeed are?'

She smiled a wry little smile as she poured out a brandy measure. She left it at Father Jude's table and took his money. Then she crossed the bar and bolted the door.

'I've just broken it off with my girlfriend,' he said after a long silence.

'I heard. Not subtle, but done.'

'Done,' he said nodding.

Silence for a few moments, then he said: 'I'm just wondering if she's going to be laughing or crying herself to sleep tonight. Don't laugh, Siobhán. Don't laugh.'

She was laughing, holding herself with trying to stop.

'Oh my God, Martin. You're some boy,' she said at last, and started into another round of laughing.

She poured another pint and joined him outside the counter, but she would not drink anything stronger than a 7 Up, and he talked, told her of his family down the country and how everything was all mixed up, and how he hoped to break free and find some place for himself in life. He rambled on about books he had read and poetry that he liked, and films, and places that he would visit if he ever found a job that would allow him the money and the time to travel. She told him that her father was an army sergeant and that she did not get on with him: trouble in the home that she would not elaborate on.

He had several pints, and Father Jude made occasional sorties from his table in the corner and joined them in chat, in which he turned everything to mathematical speculation. He would come out with all sorts of expressions that he employed in class: 'I don't give a continental, my boy,' and 'Gracious me,' and 'You don't say.' His protuberant lips and eyes in great agitation as he expounded upon the lunacy of human behaviour, much of it, he would concede, necessary to the survival of the species. Furthermore, he assured them that even the attractions between male and female and indeed all kinds of human folly could be mathematically expressed in proven computations for randomness. His enthusiasm subsided after some time and he finally made it to his table with one last effort, put his head down and slumped there muttering to himself in a dignified, comatose state.

'What am I going to do with him now?' she said. 'If he's not back in the castle soon they'll be up here looking for him.'

'We can link him down the road a bit. He'll come round in the fresh air.'

'And if he doesn't?'

'We can slip him in a window somewhere.'

She started to laugh. 'Oh Jesus.'

'Come on. After a hundred yards he'll be skipping along.'

'Martin, don't make me laugh again. Don't even talk while we do this.'

They got the old priest upright, one to each side with an arm about the shoulder and they dragged him out the door, which she locked, then on into the dark with them while his shoes scuffed along the tarmac. He was not very heavy. In linking him along their hands reached onto each other's shoulders, and it felt fine to them to be thus innocently attached. They passed along the twilit road under the spreading crowns of trees and they stood a moment at the crossroad that branched to their right between the senior pitches and the main school grounds. He suggested this way and to go in by the stile. The light of a car spread about them from behind and they shifted onto the grass margin, but the car stopped beside them and the front passenger door was thrown open and Father Paddy's face glared up from within. With urgent precision they lowered Father Jude into the passenger seat and slammed the car door shut and ran up the road and jumped the stile into the football pitches.

'Over towards the ditch,' he uttered, and they ran for the cover of a high bank of trees and bushes. They crouched in the long grass and watched the lights of the car pass up the road and turn into the college by a back entrance.

'Did he see our faces?' she asked.

'I don't know,' he answered, but he knew that Paddy's deductions were rarely off the mark. He would know all and there was no escaping it.

'Jesus, what a caper!' she said.

They were walking along under the hedges of the field, the pale outline of the goalposts standing against the night sky. The grass licked at his shoes as he stepped with a soft whispering sound, and he was aware of how close she was to him in this solitude that he could feel in his heart, as if she shared it somehow and made it bearable for him and he strong within it. They walked, and he could find little enough to say for a while, awkward, until she started up about films she had seen and places she would like to visit. Finally she faced him and said: 'I'm afraid of drink and what it does to people. Look at Father Jude. He's supposed to be one of the best mathematical brains in Europe. He's a drunk, a nicer drunk than my father, but still a drunk. I'm afraid of having a good time. That kind of thing leads nowhere. It's only a distraction. I can't risk any of that. My plan is to get out and up.'

'I want to get out of here and do things,' she said after a moment's silence. 'See places like Paris, London, the Middle East. I'd love to live in New York for a bit, see San Francisco.'

'Flowers in their hair,' he said.

She turned her eyes on him and from what she could see he seemed to know what she was talking about.

'I need to get out too,' he said. 'But first I want to see the country. I want to see Kerry and Cork, Derry and Belfast. There's a concert in Clare later in the summer. I'd like to go to it. I can't wait to see autumn in my father's fields, cattle in the mornings, the dew and the early winter frost. I haven't known any of that since I was a child.'

'God but you're a dreamer.'

He laughed at her teasing tone. But it was true nonetheless, what he'd said. He had often pondered about the farm back home with autumn dew on it and the smells of early morning in his face.

'*Touché*,' he said.

'You're a poet,' she said, taking his hand in hers. The warmth of it in his left hand, the fingers soft on his palm and his knuckles idly brushing the seam of her jeans as they strode.

'My first day here after my arrival we ran around these pitches, the cross-country team of Father Paddy.'

'You don't look like an athlete.'

'I'm not, never was. But for a few weeks I made an effort at competitive running. Then I stopped.'

'Why?'

'I felt like an eejit running behind the others. Getting ignored.'

'You were looking for encouragement.'

'I suppose that was it.'

'If you'd stayed at it, who knows?'

'Who knows? I didn't, that's all I know now.'

He looked at her sideways, saw the beauty in the semi-dark that framed about her face.

'You seem to shine in the night,' he said.

'Go on.'

'It's true.' He could see her smiling, her long graceful neck and the hair tied back.

'Those things that Father Jude was talking about. I'd like to have brains like that,' he said.

She laughed at this. 'I'll never know what you'll say next,' she said.

'I have that problem all right. The words just pop out.'

'You seem to regret things.'

'That's it. I've missed this boat. Now there's the price to pay.'

'Life is long. There's always other things.'

'True. Tomorrow a whole new world.'

'That's right, freedom.'

Then, she added: 'It's today y'know, after midnight. Today's your day of freedom.'

'Today.'

'It's one in the morning and I hate to remind you. You've got an exam in a few hours.'

'I know,' he said, and he gave her hand a gentle squeeze, and before he realised what he was doing, he was kissing her mouth, soft and deep. Her arms were warm and tight about the shirt that he wore and he could feel himself getting hard against her and she was meeting his kisses, and his tongue entered her mouth, and then his hands were undoing the clasp on her bra beneath her T shirt. Of a sudden, she pushed him off.

'Why did you do that, Martin?' she said.

'I just thought ..' was all he could manage to say.

She stood back from him. 'What I thought when I kissed you is gone now, Martin. Goodbye.'

'Siobhán, wait. Don't go. I never ...' But he could not finish the sentence. He stood there like a betrayer of some sort, condemned forever to the role of Judas, and he watched her disappear in the twilight of the field, and her shape melted like that of a ghost.

Afterward, he could not figure out how long he had stood there, like he'd been turned to a statue or a beacon of some sort, posted off some darkened shore. He sensed someone close by and he looked about.

'Martin, get to bed for heaven's sake.' Father Paddy in grim silhouette. 'The door from the swimming pool side is open,' he threw over his shoulder as he went off on another of his insomniac prowls.

He did not see her again, but she never left his mind, even years afterward. She was there: the same old wrong that he carried about inside him, always looking for a chance to ditch it, but never finding one.

He sat his final exam that morning, with the picture of her pretty face in his head and he struggled at the allegorical questions of right and wrong

91

from Shakespeare and Dickens. He knew that he was closer to what they were trying to tell him: stuff about betrayal and love and beauty gone off on some questful tangent where anything might happen for the bad by way of danger and retribution. He had a lot to learn, and a lifetime to do it.

Five years later, when once again it had all come to an end for him, and he was leaving another part of himself behind, he decided to have a look around the old battlefield of his adolescence, and he drove the seventy miles and pulled up and parked the car at the Fox's Arms. It was a fine summer day. He went inside and ordered a coffee and sandwiches for himself at the counter. He recognised Mrs Whelan right away and she smiled like she remembered him from somewhere.

'Any word of Siobhán?' he enquired.

Her face lit up. 'She sends a card at Christmas. Hasn't been home in ages. I heard that she's going to work in Saudi Arabia. After the big money. She's a nurse now.'

'That's nice,' he said. 'I'm glad.'

'You knew her I suppose.'

'I used to be a boarder in the school.'

'Ah yes. She worked there a bit.'

'I'm glad she's doing fine.'

'What's your name by the way?

'Martin,' he said. 'If you see her sometime just say hello for me.'

'I'll do that.'

He wandered up the road and crossed the grounds and walked around to the front of the castle and Father Paddy was there, like he'd been waiting for him all the time. He was sitting on a garden bench sunning himself in his habit and sandals before the front door. The hair was completely gone, but his face was the same: the healthy, rugged features of a countryman turned priest. 'Martin,' he said, looking up suddenly and his severe, old, craggy face beamed. He stood and held a hand out. They shook hands.

They sat on the summer seat side by side.

'How've you been?' Father Paddy said.

'Ah, I keep going.'

'You haven't been in touch at all.'

'The life I lead these times.'

'Yes.'

'How's Father Jude?'

Father Paddy laughed. 'All our prayers finally paid off. He hasn't drank in over a year now. God bless the old rascal. He's better than any of us now.'

'That's good. He's quite a man.'

'He mentions you sometimes, you and some girl that he calls the princess. You needn't tell me who she is. I think I know.'

They stared out across the grounds, over the golf course, not saying anything, but thinking the same things: the distance between them.

'I hope you bear no ill will towards us, Martin.'

'Of course not, Father. I grew up in this place. It made me, for better or worse.'

'I would hope that it would be the better for you.'

'Of course, me too.'

They were silent once more, an easier silence now, a shared one, fellowship somehow.

'I'm striving for peace, Martin. I pray for this peace that I experienced occasionally when I was a boy, and that comes back to me sometimes, and I pray that others also may find it. Especially these days with all these troubles in this poor old country of ours. Bombs everywhere, killings every day.'

'These days, the word peace is used in a political way.'

'I know. But politics in all its manifestations is the way of this world, and of course it is imperfect, just as people are. We must all in our different ways take on our responsibilities.' He laughed a small laugh as if at some private joke, and then he said: 'I often pray for my problem students and sometimes I pray for the occasional princess. I'm foolish enough to believe that prayer is the only thing that really counts. Much good comes of it, Martin.'

The old priest smiled, his eyes twinkling in the sunlight, like he'd just woken up to something special.

'You're a good man, Father Paddy,' was all he could think of saying at that moment, and after a long silence he said: 'You know, when I was here, all I ever wanted was to get out, to see the world.'

'That's normal enough.'

'Yeah, but I never made any plans about what exactly I would do.'

'And what did you do since that time?'

'I farmed for a few years.'

'And now?'

'Now, I'm leaving again.'

'Any particular reason?'

'Yes, but …..'

'That's fine by me, Martin. I will not probe. But with the way the country is at the moment and from what I know of you, I would say it is for either of two reasons, a girl or political. Perhaps a mixture of the two.'

'As usual, Father Paddy, you're close.'

'I'll pray for you. That's all I can do.'

'Thank you.'

'Where you thinking of going?'

'Not sure. I've cousins in America. Maybe there. I don't know yet.'

'There's a bed for you here if you want to stay a night or two.'

'That's kind of you, Father, but I think I'll move on.'

'I'm wishing you the best, Martin. Will you listen to a bit of advice?'

'Go ahead.'

The old priest had his head down, looking at his sandaled feet. Then he lifted his eyes, scanned the golf course, smiled to himself and nodded. 'Your life is your own. Make sure that your decisions are made with this foremost in mind rather than choosing the best option available. There are times when the best available is not the best one to take. You may need to wait, to work, to study. You may need to travel. Always distrust what is on offer, chances are it is not good enough, and then often, you may be stuck with the thing.'

'You're a deep one, Father Paddy.'

'We get like that, especially in these contemplative months before the boys arrive in the autumn. We are plunged into the thick of it then, running the school. Just remember what I told you about making your life your own.'

'Do you think I'll ever meet her again, Father?'

'The princess?'

'Yes.'

'Who knows? Sometimes, fate takes a hand too. Things get lost and other things get found. Life is full of trials and marvels like that.'

'I've left everything, Father. That's why I've come here, the farm, the girl I'm engaged to. Everything.'

'If there is no going back then, you must start again from nothing.'

'Not easy.'

'Not easy. You will have to be inventive as well as brave.'

'Yes,' he said.

Edge of the World

She moved closer to the bed, found her jeans lying on the floor beside it. She pulled them on, shoved her nightie down into them, dragged on a pullover and her socks and runners. She went downstairs to the kitchen and half-filled and switched on the electric kettle. A coffee was what she needed. He could be back anytime, anytime. The dread that he might not; she pushed it away, sat at the kitchen table and listened to the kettle come to the boil.

I'm not waiting for him, she told herself. Not. I'm up because I can't sleep. That's all, and because I am no longer a sensible person, I can do this and it is all right. It was not the first time he'd left her on one of her weekend visits. Something really urgent, he'd told her. It was just the first time she'd woken up at his house with him gone and she unable to sleep.

He was right when he'd told her how time seemed to stretch during a sleepless night. He'd said that maybe it had something to do with the absence of light if the explanation for it was physical, or maybe it was due to the powerful solitude of the graveyard hours. He'd told her things like this: unsensible things, in an attempt to explain himself. Always artful in his use of language, like a sudden slip might expose something that he could never want her to see, and yet he was compelled to explain.

He always talked around things, invoking, suggesting, like no other way would suffice to describe what he had to do when he left her of a sudden; always by the back of the house, to where a car lay waiting to pick him up a half mile or so away. Then, off with him. She would be left with just the smile as he turned for the door, half apologetic, reluctance and eagerness competing in his step, a casual goodbye, the backdoor clicking, the sound of footsteps on the stones of the yard. Quietness then in the old farmhouse.

She sipped at her coffee, could feel its quiet lift, like a soft tongue down the sides of her throat, a faint quickening of breath and heartbeat, her fingers finding heat on the contours of the mug.

97

It occurred to her to leave a note before going out to say that she was only gone for a walk in case he returned in her absence, but she decided against it. Let him wait and wonder if he must. She would take her walk, go out the back door and cross the yard as he had done, but she would head for the beach.

The sky pale dark overhead, an early winter sky with daylight filtering from other time zones over the tilt of the earth and the blackthorn hedges on either side of the road. She walked with her hands stuck into the side-pockets of an old denim jacket of his, head down anxious to get off the road in case a car came along: a curious neighbour who would surely stop and enquire if she was all right. She cut down the boreen towards the strand, and after a few minutes of walking she could taste the sea air in her breathing, enticing on her face. She detected the wash of wave on sand and hurried her steps.

The car was parked at the end of the boreen on the very sand of the beach and she walked right against it before discerning what it was, slapping at the bonnet as she stumbled. The door opened. A torch shone in her face.

'Guard,' she said.

Standing at the open door of the car, he said: 'Miss Russell,' and turned his torch away.

'Guard Foran,' he said, introducing himself.

'Lovely night, Guard,' she said.

'Yes. Nice out here.'

'I couldn't sleep.'

'Lucky you. I was finding it hard to stay awake.'

She gave a polite giggle and made to pass on by. He had the torch aimed at his feet now, a small circle of light about his shoes, the rest of him all silhouette.

'Miss Russell,' he said. 'What brought you here?'

'None of your business, Guard Foran, but if you must know, curiosity.'

'We're only ten miles from the border, Miss Russell. Curiosity is a dangerous thing over these parts. The man you're staying with is a known republican activist.'

'I'm aware of that. I'm interested in the current conflict and John is a close friend of mine as well as a useful source of research for me. I'm a historian as you probably know.'

She turned once more to walk on.

'Miss Russell,' he said then.

'Yes?'

'There are some aspects to my work that I don't enjoy. I hope you understand that.'

'I know that, Guard Foran.'

'Thank you, Miss Russell. Now I never saw you here tonight and you never saw me. I'd be grateful if we kept this close.'

'Certainly, Guard Foran.'

She walked on. The encounter made her smile. No doubt he had been sent out to watch the house and headed for the beach instead, a decent sort, caught up in the times that were in it and not liking it a bit.

The sea washed at the sand close to her feet, and a yellow blade of crescent moon glinted on the surface of the water, and she walked and walked and walked.

From the road she knew he was back, she could sense it, and crossing the yard she could detect the quiet hum of the washing machine, telling her of his need to wash away forensic traces of whatever it was he had been up to. He stood in the kitchen dressed in a blue tracksuit, half turned to her, barefoot, his hair wet and he, smelling of shower gel.

'You gave me a fright, Cathy,' he said.

'Me being gone?'

'Yeah.'

'I'm reassured, John.'

He smiled happily. Handsome bastard.

'How'd it go?'

'Fine.'

'I was afraid, John.'

'Me too.'

'I find that hard to believe.'

'Since I met you I've got like that.'

'Love me like you'll never see me again, like you'll never love me again. Love me like that.'

'Oh God,' he said, like he was afraid.

She stood waiting for him, the arms about her then, and the kisses, his hands everywhere, pushing her clothes off, taking her to the floor, cold under her at first, then the mad lovemaking. Her cries became something like laughing that she found hard to stop even after they had climaxed and stopped and sat up looking at each other naked, smiling and amazed.

'It's never been like this before,' he said. 'Must be the adrenalin.'

They dressed, sat at the table and drank coffee and had a breakfast, and the kitchen warmed up some after he plugged in an electric heater. She told him about the guard.

'He asked me to keep it quiet,' she said.

'A decent poor devil, but if I make a slip he'll get me put in jail.'

'He doesn't want to do that.'

'No, but he'll do his job.'

'And you'll do yours.'

He nodded. 'Until the last of the Brits are gone from the North I'll be after them.' He hung his head a moment, looking away. He turned his glance towards her. 'When are you off?'

'Three in the afternoon. I've a long drive, a heap of lectures tomorrow.'

'Do you teach them anything about this?'

'It's not on the course that I do.'

'Is it on any course?'

'Kind of.'

'That's us, kind of, but not quite. We're off the limits of public perception. Off the edge of the bloody world.'

'That's not true, John. Let's not argue about it.'

He said nothing for a moment, then: 'I'll go crazy until you come back.'

'You'll be fine.'

He nodded, smiled. 'You still on the pill?'

'Yeah.'

'Maybe we should try for a child.'

She shook her head. 'I don't know how I could do it. Give up lecturing. Come out here to live full time.'

'We're in love. Marry me.'

'You know I'd do it but ….'

'But what?'

'The fear, John. It's good for lovemaking. But a child? How could we have a child in this scenario?' She was looking right at him.

'A lot of families have to.'

'They have no choice across the border. We have on this side. This whole thing has gone on since the time of Strongbow. You're not going to tell me that we can have kids when it's all over in a year or two.'

'If people thought like that we'd have disappeared as a race long ago.'

'I couldn't bring a baby into this feeling that I got earlier when I woke up in bed and you were out with your comrades somewhere, trying to kill someone or maybe getting killed yourselves.'

'We'll keep our family safe. I've not brought anything home since you arrived and none of my friends have either.'

'You don't understand, John. The idea that you could be killed. Maybe you think you can live with that, but I don't think I can. This thing that we push to the back of our minds: what I felt earlier, a kind of greyish feeling.'

'Cathy, you're my beacon of light on a dark and stony road.'

'John, I can't join you in this. It's being planned and fought from our living rooms and our dinner tables. Even with children in our arms it's in us, the next operation, the last one, the danger that keeps you alert, keeps you afraid, keeps you angry inside. How could we protect children from that?'

'I thought you sympathised.'

'I do.'

'Marry me. Have our babies.'

'Not the way things are now, John. Not with this fear.'

'Is there no hope for us then?'

STRAY DOG

He was convalescing after a car accident and things were bad in the house: the biggest house around and not a spare penny in it. He had come home to this: the ruin of his father's affairs. His mother kept her head down to the housework and her calves when she wasn't bickering with his father and blaming him for the mess that they were all in. He wanted to leave again but his back was too weak. He dragged himself about the farm repairing things, doing small jobs.

He thought he might qualify for social welfare in Dublin if he used the address of a friend and he managed that stroke: taking the bus up once a week and signing on at an employment exchange on the Navan Road and getting the bus back. With some of the money he bought a battery for the old 135 Massey Ferguson tractor and changed the oil filter and fuel filters and got it going again. He managed to get their Fiat 127 car insured and back on the road with the tax disc from one of the tractors stuck on its windscreen.

Every second day, threatening letters from the bank arrived, interest of eighteen percent accumulating onto a fortune owed at the rate of a thousand pounds a month. He walked beside his father up the street one of the days, feeling more than ever a hostage to family misfortune. There were years abroad when at least he had a memory of rock-solid mooring points. Not now. A storm of some sort had broken up all that, and he was back amid the ruin. His father greeted to his left and his right friends and neighbours that they passed, his head down much of the time as they neared the bank. Into the building then, and they stood waiting to see the manager, ignoring the smirks of some of the bank staff. The manager appeared after some minutes, a small man with a thin face, and he beckoned them into his office and led the way. They sat in front of a desk and the manager sat behind it with his elbows on the surface and his fingers entwined.

His father then outlined his concerns regarding repayment of his debts and gave assurances that he would get things on the level again given time. He cut in on his father then. 'The letters will have to stop,' he said. 'We want them stopped.'

The manager looked surprised, expecting anything but this, nodded, detecting anger, menace.

After that, the letters to the house stopped. It became easier going in at dinner-time without the demands to pay waiting on the table.

Still he saw no light ahead, and when money allowed, he, his brother and father would go up the town some of the nights and bury their troubles at the counter of King's bar. They would talk and his father would go over the yarns that they'd heard so often before. But his father was a broken chieftain now and his clan impoverished. 'It'll all wear away,' his father would say sometimes. It was like he was talking to himself and not to his two sons. They would listen and smile and bite back on the bitterness they felt.

His mother was not one to wait. At the dinner table one day, she told the whole family of her plan.

'I think we should invite old Paddy home,' she said.

No one said anything. 'Sure he was in the navy. He must have two pensions,' she added. 'If we mind him here, I'm sure he'll pay his way. He might even have savings that he could leave us.'

'I suppose,' his father said then.

'I'll send him the usual card at Christmas with a little note in it. I'm sure he'd like to spend his final years with his people.'

'We need the money,' his father said, and he got up from the table and went outside to the yard.

'What do you think?' his brother said. They were outside in one of the sheds putting a handle in a hayfork.

'Maybe it's our last chance.'

'Having that man in the house,' his brother said then, and he shook his head.

104

'We've had him before.'

'A week or two every few years. Different in the house week after week. The ancient fucking mariner.'

'In trouble and never out of trouble,' he quoted to his brother from one of Paddy's letters.

'I hate Mondays. Broke my knee on a Monday,' the brother quoted then in his best effort at a Scouse accent. They laughed.

The new scheme put his mother at the controls. The card and letter were sent off and there were phone calls from Liverpool over the next while. 'Ello luv,' when he lifted the receiver some of the evenings. Paddy was warming to the idea. His mother was playing him along: hauling in the line. Paddy's annual Christmas card and letter arrived one day. Three wise men with camels on a hill, the star of Bethlehem overhead and on the card the legend: A Time of Hope. The letter was read aloud: another classic in abject melancholia.

Afterwards in the yard, he asked his father: 'What's our connection with Paddy?'

'He's my father's cousin. He was fostered in our house after his parents died.'

'Why did he leave?'

'He was selling spuds on the side. Hanging out with a bad crowd up the town. The old man wouldn't have it. Sent him packing.'

'When?'

'A few months before the Tans burned the town.'

'But he's ok now I suppose.'

'He's headed on for eighty. He's as good as he'll ever be.'

It seemed like the idea was just short of being right: like signing on the dole in Dublin. You did anything to survive, he supposed. Some days he came upon his father, seeing him close to tears standing by one of the outhouses, like he was watching for something that refused to happen no matter how much it was prayed for.

There were days after foddering the cattle in the slatted shed when he sat in the tractor cab with the engine turned off and watched through the raised front-loader the winter darkness come down over the fields like a slow misty waterfall, and he rested his eyes over the spread of country to the north, up towards Leitrim, Cavan, Fermanagh. He loved the fields and the lonesome calls of cattle in wintertime that were taking him back to better days before family fortunes went down. Escape seemed the only option, but there was no money and his injuries would take at least a year to heal; if they ever did.

His younger sister spoke of leaving for America. But where would she get the money? He pondered like there was a fortune in those depths that his father seemed forever to stare into.

His mother in the cow byre one evening with the bucket of milk for the house beside her, her face all upset.

'I lost my ring,' she said.

He knew the ring well. It was a gold ring encrusted all the way around with diamonds: a present from his father in better times. She gave the cow a slap along the back and drove her out of the byre.

'Would you try to find it?' she said.

He looked at the byre floor. It was covered in a deep level of cowdung and bedding. The ring was down there somewhere.

'I'll have a look,' he said.

His mother walked off with her bucket of milk and he got onto his hunkers and started to feel around in the cowdung with his fingers. After a minute he gave up on the search. Everything about the chore asked of him said no. It seemed like his entire life was down there in the cow slurry with that damned ring. He straightened up and went outside and washed his hands at a tap.

Paddy phoned one evening, saying he would be over on the ferry the following day and could someone meet him. His mother said sure, and took down the details. Next day his father drove up.

That afternoon, he did nothing much, just sat at the window to the yard.

'How do you think it'll go?' he asked his mother.

'He's worth a try,' she answered.

'How long will you give him?'

She looked around like he'd said something obscene.

'The things you say to me now,' she said.

He could find nothing to respond.

Towards tea time, the car entered the yard, and his father carried two suitcases into the kitchen. Paddy walked behind, dragging his bad leg. He wore a suit. He stood in the middle of the floor and shook hands with them all.

'You must be starving, Paddy,' his mother said.

'I am a bit,' Paddy answered, and he laughed politely and passed the cigarettes around and they all smoked except his father, and chatted.

His mother served up steak with onions, mushrooms, tea and soda bread. That night the men, walked up the town to King's bar and had a small welcome home party for Paddy and introduced him to some of the locals. Paddy made enquiries of old acquaintances; most of them were dead, and some who were not drank in other bars further up the street.

'That's the trouble of being away,' Paddy said. 'You've been away yourself your father tells me.'

'Yeah, Europe.'

'France?'

'That's right.'

'Docked there a few times. How'd you find the French women?'

'Cold.'

'How's that?'

'I was broke a lot of the time.'

Paddy laughed. 'The old story,' he said.

'I married two times,' he said then.

'They die?'

'Died. My family's gone. A daughter in Australia. A son in New Zealand.'

Paddy paused in his chat, looked around him at the others playing darts up along the bar.

He watched Paddy's old head sidelong, the grey hair and the skin loose and faded, the freckles of his youth barely visible, the eyes lustful still: an ugly face that revealed a lack of moorings in his life and the heavings of strange decks underfoot.

'Ever miss this place, Paddy?'

'Not since your grandfather drove me in the trap to the train station in nineteen twenty. A long time ago, that was. Wasn't much to miss really.'

'You've travelled a bit.'

'Merchant seaman. Sure.'

'The war?'

'Yeah. I had a few close calls all right. Was on the Atlantic convoys.'

'Got a pension?'

He laughed. 'Your mother asked me that. Yeah, it keeps me going.'

Paddy seemed to fit in well about the house, and they got used to his complaining about the weather all the time and the aches in his bad knee and the way he wheezed, so loud in his sleep that they could hear it out on the landing.

One of the wintry days, when mists hang over the sheds and the trees about the house, he sits with Paddy in the kitchen smoking, while his mother does the dishes at the sink and a friend of his mother comes into the kitchen from the yard and walks across the floor. Paddy's undisguised look of hunger follows the woman in her strides, and his mother says then: 'A man of your years.'

He watches Paddy get up and go out the door, and on up the pass towards the road. Paddy stops at the gate to light a cigarette before turning and heading on for the town.

Even if Things are not Normal

She looks up and around. He is standing in the doorway from the hall, his eyes on her, gentle and puzzled-looking.

'You could at least have knocked.'

'I didn't want to wake youse. Didn't know you were up.'

'Did you not see the light?'

'I did but you often leave it on.'

'I do.'

'That's why I didn't knock.'

'Considerate of you, Shane. Make a coffee if you want.'

'I will thanks.'

He moves across the sitting room and goes into the tiny kitchen. She can hear him moving things about. She gets up, goes over to the window and draws aside one of the curtains.

'I can see the Black Mountain. Daylight soon,' she says.

She looks out at the street where nothing is stirring, and at the dark mountain over Belfast that has a veil of mist about its flanks like a huge cobweb. There is light in the windows across the way. She reckons that all the parents are up, and have not slept this night. She turns back into the room.

'Where were youse playin'?' she says.

'The Felons' Club.'

'A good night?'

'It was fine. Met some of the lads afterwards.'

'And you decided to just call by. Nice of you.'

'For God's sakes, Deirdre. I know it's her first day at school.'

'Is this visit for our daughter's sake or is it because you need to prove something?'

He comes into the room and hands her a mug of coffee. She sits on the sofa once more and takes a sip. He lowers himself into an armchair.

'You been sleeping ok these times?' he says.

'I take the pills. Earlier in the summer I was fine. Getting closer to the time I just couldn't. It's the old fear back again. I thought when the ceasefire came it would go and it did for a while. This summer it came back.'

'We need to act normal.'

'Aye, I know.'

'I get nightmares myself sometimes thinkin' I'm back in the Blocks. We were playing in Amsterdam in July and I had some bad nights then. When I'm back here I meet the lads all the time and I feel better. Dunno why that is.'

'PTS, Shane. Ever hear of it?'

'I know what it is. I can even describe it for you.'

'Maybe you should do something about it.'

'Maybe.'

'Oh, I give up. Why do I waste my concern on someone who in his head is still living in a H Block wing with all his mates.'

'We won't go over this again.'

'No, Shane. But I will say this. Our generation carried the fight. Our children are now in the front line. Our innocent little children.'

She looks away from him and drinks deep at her coffee. 'Oh, this day has been waiting for us since the minute she was born.' She starts to cry, a hand to her forehead. Some coffee spills onto her jeans. He comes over, kneels beside her.

'We're together on this, Deirdre. Ok?'

He waits until she stops crying. She takes up her mug and sips again at the coffee.

'We'll be normal even if things are not,' he says. 'A child's first day at school is a big event. If things get bad I'll cover her eyes.'

'You'll have to cover her ears too.'

'If we have to.'

'They sing a little song going up the road. She's been learning it from a

110

tape that the school sent out. Keeps their minds off those men shouting their filthy abuse at them.'

'A good idea.'

'It's not right you know. There's no one to speak up for us except ourselves. I was asked in the incident centre by a journalist from the South if it was true that some of the parents had been convicted of terrorist offences.'

'What did you say?'

'I told him it was true and asked him if full-grown men terrorising little girls on their way to school was not terrorism and if it might have him thinking as to why we fought in the first place. Oh, what difference? He didn't want to know anything beyond making criminals of us all.'

'We need to be calm, Deirdre. That's all we can do for the moment. What time is it?'

'Half seven. I'll get her up. She'll be happy you're here.'

'Does she know what it'll be like?'

'I've told her a bit.'

'I heard the police called round last night.'

'They called to all the parents.'

'Snipers waiting for us I heard.'

'That's what they said.'

'I've thought about this, Deirdre, whether my presence will be a danger to you both or not. If you don't want me to walk with you I won't. Tell me.'

'Ask her, Shane. She'll tell you herself.'

She leaves the sitting room and goes upstairs. He stands at the window facing the street. The Black Mountain is fully visible now beyond the rooftops, and he allows himself memories of being up there courting girls in cars when he was a teenager and the Troubles were only just starting. He'd even taken Deirdre up there after his release from prison twenty years afterward. He supposes that his daughter was conceived under the slopes of that mountain.

A convoy of armoured personnel carriers and landrovers rumbles along the street and he watches, waiting for the tail of it to pass the house. Protection of a sort, a token effort, he reckons. A helicopter clatters beyond the roofs and he looks up at it, wondering if the display of military saturation will dissuade the snipers. He hears the patter of his daughter's footsteps on the stairs. He turns, waiting for her to appear in the doorway of the sitting room, forming a smile on his face.

THE BELT

The heartache of his childhood came back to haunt him as he mounted the hospital stairs; it forewarned him of an old stammer, the smell of his father's smoking, and the shop. Always twilight in the shop, even in summertime, until the late afternoon, and the sun low to the west beyond the town flooded inside, throwing its shadows from an ESB pole and the petrol pumps in through the large shop window.

His sister at the door of the public ward smiled at his approach. She kissed him on the side of his face.

'He's over to the left,' she said. 'They have a screen drawn.'

'How is he?'

'Conscious mostly. He could slip away any time or he could last for a day or two yet.'

He looked long at her: that permanently sad face, the picture of his mother as he remembered.

'How've you been?' he said.

'Good enough. Sure there's nothing we can do except wait.'

'Yes,' he said.

He'd come straight from work, a sports jacket pulled on in a hurry. He undid his blue tie and stuffed it into a pocket.

'Sean,' she said, putting a hand to his shoulder. 'Try not to be hard on him.'

'What's the use now?' he said.

He went into the ward and immediately saw the area to the left screened off. He walked over. His father there on a bed, propped up on pillows, labouring in his efforts to breathe.

'It's me, Dad,' he said, sitting down.

His father's eyes flickering for a moment, the old, yellow face turned on the pillow.

'It's me, Dad. Sean.'

'Good of you to come,' his father said, in a voice that was little more than a whisper.

'Dad, I, I, I . . . . . .'

'That old stammer. You've still got it.'

'S S Sometimes.'

'I was hoping . . . . you'd grow . . . . .out of it.'

'Yes.'

'I'm finished you know. Finished.'

'It's ok.'

'For you it may be. Not for me.'

'Yes.'

'You see why I hated you to smoke.'

You hated me, Dad, smoking or not. The last time you used the belt on me was for smoking. You hated me.

'Yes,' he said again.

'Lifetime of it. My lungs ruined. Every breath, agony.'

'Take it easy.'

The heavy breathing of his father, the nebulizer blowing that stream up his nostrils. *My father is like someone dead in mysterious circumstances. I have no wish to piece it all together, to draw up a scenario of last known movements.*

'How's the children?'

'They're fine, Dad. Why don't you take it easy there?'

'I'll be taking it easy soon enough. Tell me. . . . . your family.'

'They're all good. Doing well at school. May is doing a bit of part time teaching.'

'Good.'

I find it hard to talk to you. Your throat on fire with cancer. By rights I should talk and you listen. The real things I want to say to you. The real things. No wonder I had a stammer. Will you acknowledge what you did to me?

'How's the work?'

'Fine.'

'Not easy being a guard . . . . .these days.'

'No, but the pay's all right.'

'Yes.'

'Being a sergeant makes it easier. A quiet little town where we are.'

'Good.'

He thought he detected a smile on his father's face, not much of a smile: the few teeth bared momentarily.

'I was proud of you, Sean. The Scott Medal. Not many get it.'

'I did what was expected of me. Nothing more.' *I never knew where the courage came from. Was it courage at all? The pistol pointed at me. Talking to the lad, seeing the doubt in his eyes: that maybe he would not shoot. Facing the belt was worse.*

'The Guards ………..made a man of you.'

'Yes.'

'I wanted you to know I was proud……… Your name in the papers.'

'Ah, I dunno.'

'The whole town was talking about it. They'd come into the shop. Stopping an armed robbery on his own, they'd say……… It made me proud of you.'

'That's good.' *I could have been shot. But it didn't happen. I was lucky after all the years. Lucky.*

'I have a favour to ask you, Sean.'

'Sure. Ask.'

'The kids. I'd like to see them. Why didn't you bring them?'

I thought you were going to ask me to forgive you.

'A hundred miles, Dad. I just took off and drove here. I'll get May to bring them in the morning.'

'I'll hold on for that.'

'You'll be fine, Dad.'

'Stop saying that, will you?'

A touch of the old anger. In the old days a thrashing for the least untruth. The belt off then.

'I'll have them here in the morning, first thing.'

'That'll .... be nice.'

'Yes.'

'A pity you never brought them before. Life is short, Sean.'

'Yes, Dad.'

'Your mother would be proud of you .... and them.'

It wore her down in the end. A broken heart killed her. Watching you beating me. Not being able to stop you.

'I think you should try to sleep, Dad.'

'Don't go far.'

'I won't. Sheila or myself will be here. And you'll have May and the kids first thing in the morning.'

'I'll look forward to that. Seeing them at last. Yes.'

'Try to rest, Dad.'

'Yes. And then I'll try to wake up again.' An attempt at humour. He turned his old face away and closed his eyes then.

'A rest will do you good, Dad. Try to rest. I'm going out for a cup of coffee.'

He walked from the ward and found his sister looking out a window on the corridor.

'Sheila,' he said.

'Well?'

'He asked to see the kids.'

'And what did you say?'

'I said they'll be here in the morning.'

'You're doing the right thing, Sean.'

'After all he did to me, he asks for this. I was stupid to think he might ask for forgiveness.'

'That's his loss, not yours. This is not a time for anger, Sean.'

'Maybe I was hoping he'd see the wrong he did. I even started to stutter again.'

'I feel sorry for him. He beat me too, you know.'

'I know that. But he seemed to have a preference for me.'

'I remember. Let's try and let it all die with him. That's all we can do.'

What could be said? he wondered. How much of it all would die with his father? They sat in the canteen, he and his sister across from each other at a formica-topped table. Late in the evening now, shadows beyond the windows across the grounds outside. He thought of the shop. He felt that it would be such a relief to get into his car and drive away. Drive home. Go into the kids' room while they slept and kiss their faces. Get into bed then. Kiss his sleeping wife on the shoulder and lie back.

'I don't know what brought me here,' he said.

'Your sense of right, Sean.'

'I feel nothing for him, you know. Nothing.'

'His father may have beaten him too.'

'It doesn't excuse.'

'No, it doesn't.' He put his head down for a moment, took a sip of his coffee then.

'How's the work?' his sister said.

'All right.'

'Isn't it funny, Sheila?' he said after a long silence. 'The things that are foremost in your head are often the very things that you can't speak about.'

'Did you ever talk to May about him?'

'No. No one.'

'Counselling might help.'

'I know. Maybe after everything is over.'

'You should, Sean. You should do that. Promise me.'

'Ok.'

He stared at his sleeping father for a long time, watched the breath lift and drop the frail chest beneath the bedcovers. It seemed strong enough, the breathing, though laboured. A day or two yet. In the morning he would have to phone up the superintendent. Compassionate leave. Not the right term for this kind of vigil. He felt no compassion at all; it was like watching a stranger. A nurse appeared at his side towards eleven o'clock.

'We have a room for him now,' she said. 'Just down the corridor.'

'Good.'

'We'll wheel him down. You might just clear out his locker for us.'

'Sure, I'll do that.'

He began with the top drawer: a box of disposable hankies, a wallet and some change, a toilet bag, a small box of sweets, a pack of cards, a missal, rosary beads. He swept them all into his father's overnight bag and pulled open the second drawer and immediately saw the leather belt coiled on top of the small pile of folded clothes. He picked it up, studied it a moment, held it to his face, smelled at the leather, ran a finger along the shiny, brown surface. How many times had it come down on his bare skin? More times than he could count, or wished to. All those years and seasons of bed-wetting and fear. He sat down.

His father had been wheeled out. He was alone now and everyone else in the ward was sleeping. He could not help the sobbing that rose in his chest and brought the tears, and when a nurse put a hand onto his shoulder he looked up and saw the compassion there in her young features.

'Get rid of this for me, please,' he said. 'Throw it in the rubbish. Destroy it if you can.'

She took the belt from his hand and walked away with it, out of the public ward. He got up then and finished clearing out the other drawers and followed her to the room where his father lay.

GROWING PAINS

He would watch her as she did the dishes, leaning forward over the sink, so unlike his mother, although she did the same work of cooking, washing, tidying while his mother seemed all taken up with his infant brother and sister. That was Veronica, a girl. During the first couple of months since she arrived in the house he'd been at school, only seeing her for short whiles in the evening. She came from the terrace, his mother explained to him. But he knew her younger brother who was in his class at school: a wild young lad with sly ways about him.

She always seemed happy, floating by him with piles of clothes for the wash or the ironing. She had a nice face and always carried a discreet bouquet of soap and cleanliness about her, so that even with his eyes closed he knew if she was near or had been.

He fell sick and was kept from school, a luxury being sick, if he were not so caught up in the chest and weak in his legs, and she would attend to him like he was her own brother. He sat by the range most days. It was springtime, his brothers and sisters at school, his mother coming and going, and his father off somewhere or other, like he always was. He read books and comics, and the comics were mostly war stories and cowboy adventures, and sometimes Veronica sat across from him and read one too.

'Lots of fighting,' she said to him one day. 'You'll be a soldier yet.'

It had become a standing joke.

'Oh, I don't know,' he answered, in a weak and sleepy tone of voice. He was coughing a lot, not at all like the heroes that he was reading about, and as if picking up on his thoughts, she said: 'I'm sure those boys got colds too. Just in the stories it wouldn't fit in too good, so it doesn't get mentioned.'

'Could be,' he answered. 'I never did read about any that were sick except wounded from fighting or stuff.'

She asked him if he wanted tea and he said that he did, not for the tea, but to have her near him, so that they could talk some more. It became something of a ritual most days, and his mother did not mind to see them sitting, drinking tea together at the range. He found the mornings long, especially if he were feeling feverish. He would pretend to be better than he was in order to get downstairs.

On sunny days she accompanied him for short walks to the garden, down by the sheds of the yard, by the pots of his mother's geraniums and a rose bush beginning to bud near a wall. In one of the sheds one day, he showed her his hideout, where he kept the gear that he used to arm himself with for his expeditions down the fields: wooden swords, spears, bows and arrows and even a few wooden shields. He was embarrassed somewhat, but still happy to show her the things that he had only recently grown out of. They walked around the garden by the hedge, and he felt the need to confess to some of the advantages of being sick: having things done for you, no homework or school, at home with his books and comics, keeping himself warm by the range all day.

'You'll be strong soon enough,' she told him.

He doubted it, and told her that ever since he had had his appendix out, he was prone to colds and flu, the fevers and nightmares that he got sometimes, and even pneumonia once. She insisted, saying: 'You'll grow out of it all,' and she laughed.

'In a little while you'll be running after girls like me and wanting to kiss them.'

'Never,' he said.

'You'll see, you'll see. And they'll want to kiss you,' she said then, and laughed at his look of amazement. Even in his disbelief, he knew from her face that what she had said carried some merit, though he would not admit it.

In the evenings, she would be gone home, and his brothers and sisters round him altered everything back to the old familiar: the kitchen warm and smelling of cooked food, the TV going, or sometimes not going, depending on what his mother considered suitable viewing. He had his comics and his books from the library and sometimes he played with the younger children, crawled about with them and hid behind furniture, or drew with chalk on the tiles of the floor, roads, farms, rivers and mountains where toy cars and trains might be made go. He overheard some of the adult talk, and sometimes it concerned her.

'A great young one,' his mother assured his father. Listening to them sometimes, he was able to detect much of the bleakness of adult considerations and he would lose interest in the words and phrases that seemed to lead across an unimagined place of vague uncertainties.

He always cocked an ear at any mention of her name. He heard his mother say one evening: 'She's great altogether. No bother to her to change nappies or do anything I ask her. Next time I'm in Mullingar I think I'll get her a few bits of clothes. Maybe a nice dress. She'll be dancing soon. She'll need something decent to go out in.'

His father assented as he always did and said: 'Sure you might get yourself a bit of jewellery.'

'We might do that,' his mother answered. 'I need something to match a cream blouse that I got last time. Some little gold chain maybe.'

He knew well the scenario: his parents dressed to travel and driving off, a minder in the house, usually a relative. This time it would be Veronica. He hoped he would not be brought. It seemed unlikely and only possible if his mother thought he needed something.

He looked forward to the day and counted off each one eagerly. Having her to himself seemed to be too good to happen, and it turned out so. He was left to his own devices by the range while she did the chores and flew about the house like she hadn't a minute to spare, and she had not, for she had to cope with her own work, plus that usually done by his mother. All he could do was sit and watch and try not to appear too much at a loss.

In the days that followed, he became aware of distances before him much greater than all that he had covered on his walks to school and his expeditions across fields: the painful deficit of his experience, the strange flights that his fantasy took sometimes, the new stirrings of his own body. He became awkward, more conscious of his words in her company.

Soon after, on a Sunday night before his parents and siblings, she did a pirouette on the kitchen floor in her new outfit. She was on her way to the dancehall, her first dance ever, and he thought she seemed like a film star in her make-up, with her dark hair done up, her eyes flashing and her cheeks all pretty and strange looking. He forced a smile as she shone in the new awareness of her teenage beauty, and it was as much as he could manage to keep himself from crying in front of them all there and then.

WARRIORS

These days the sun is hot, burning our arms, our legs and the back of our necks when we are on the march. We train harder than ever, running around the Barrack Field until we have to lie down and rest and for ages we all watch the blue sky roll by overhead. Then we get up and do some more training, running, crawling, wrestling in the grass.

There are times that I worry. So I have to be prepared. That's what it means to be in charge, to be leader. These lads trust me, so I have to see that they are always ready for fight at a moment's notice. We are planning a hide, off beyond the town, a place where we can be safe, where we can store our weapons and stuff, a place where we can strike out from and retreat to. It will take time and careful preparation. I warn them all to keep their mouths shut outside of the group. Only ourselves, I tell them, making sure that they listen, making sure that they understand.

I have made Glancy my second in command. I had to do it. He was beginning to talk against me and put in his own ideas, and make remarks about things I'd say. I had the choice of kicking him out or taking him in as second to me. He is popular with the others so I took the chance and he is pleased with that. He tells me things now, so I think I have him tied in. Still, I need to watch him in a sly way that he won't notice. He tells me that there are enemy camped outside the town and we should ambush them.

'How many?' I say.

'Don't know.'

'We need to know,' I tell him.

'Maybe if there are too many we won't ambush them,' he says, and he is smiling just a small bit so the others will see it and smile too, behind my back.

'I don't care if there are hundreds,' I say then. 'We still need to see how strong they are beforehand.'

I know now that I have a problem. I have to follow my own plans, not Glancy's. If I take a small group to scout the camp, he will work against me with the ones I leave behind. If we all go, there will be too many of us and we will be seen. I decide to do the scout with Glancy, just the two of us. I can see on his face that he is happy with that. He thinks that he is equal to me. Well let him think it.

We leave the other lads in the Barrack Field and we cross the wall at the back of it and head off across the fields away from the town. I let Glancy lead. He knows the way to the enemy camp. He is a bit annoyed that I did not let him bring a weapon. We need to appear innocent if we are seen. He knows I am right, but he doesn't like it.

A mile north of the town we spot the camp: clothes drying on a ditch by the roadside, a couple of canvas tents with horses and some dogs and goats tied up, and two caravans that have green barrel roofs. We crawl closer through a meadow of high grass. I can smell the stick fires, a smell I always liked. I can see long-haired women with shawls walking about. I hear the sound of children. 'We're close enough,' I say really low.

'We can hardly see anything,' Glancy says.

'We've seen enough,' I say, and I feel like thumping him now. He shuts up for a minute and I peep out again from the grass. The ditch along the road is about half a field away. We'd be right on the camp if we go any closer. This enemy is not too strong, I decide to myself. We can ambush them all right if they go through town. I lower my head.

'We'll head back,' I say. 'Come on.'

We crawl back through the long grass of the meadow and when we reach the ditch we find two boys looking at us surprised as we are. They have loops of wire in their hands and sticks and two dead rabbits that the bigger boy has tucked under an arm. They wear raggedy long trousers and jumpers and wellingtons that are too big on their feet.

'Enemy,' says Glancy to me very low. 'We're trapped.'

The two boys are bigger than us but not by much. I notice the smell of the camp fire from them.

'Hello,' I say, getting up. Glancy gets up too. They stare at us for a good while. Then the bigger boy says with a strong west of Ireland accent: 'What are youse doin'?'

'Scouting,' I say, and I look right at him, but not in a way that lets him know that I am afraid or looking for a fight either.

'Scoutin' what?' he says then, and I can see that he is puzzled by the word. I just lift my shoulders.

'For rabbits?' he says then.

'Yeah,' I say. 'Rabbits.'

'Where's yer snares?' the younger one says then.

'We're just looking,' I say.

'Come on then,' the bigger boy says. 'You can hunt with us.'

I look at Glancy and I am glad to see that he's scared chicken, all shaking like he is dying for a pee and can't go for one. I decide to drag the thing out.

'Ok,' I say.

The two boys lead the way, and after a bit of walking we find a rabbit hole and they show us how to set a snare so that the rabbit gets caught by the neck going in or out, and is held because the other end of the snare is tied to a tree root.

'That's how you do it,' the little one says. 'That's how you catch dinner,' and he points over at the two dead rabbits that the other boy is holding by the legs.

'Are they nice?' I ask. He licks his lips right around with his tongue and I know what he means.

'Are you lads brothers?' I ask.

'We are,' the bigger one says. He leads off towards another burrow, and when we get there we see that there is a rabbit caught and he is making a lot of struggles, jumping and trying to escape. His eyes are wild because he knows he will die now and he is all shaking when he stops jumping.

'More dinner,' the smaller boy says.

The bigger boy grabs the rabbit and catches him by the hind legs and lifts him so that the head is resting on the ground and then he rises the stick that he has in his other hand and whacks the rabbit with it, right on the head. He takes off the snare then and sets it again around the burrow.

'Maybe another one tomorrow,' he says.

His younger brother giggles. I notice that they have their ways of talking to each other that are quiet and easy like adults, and it makes me wonder if they know how to play, or if they ever did. Glancy is all quiet and nervous, and at the next rabbit hole he starts to tug at my clothes, interrupting me when I am asking the boys about how to cook a rabbit. It makes me wish I'd come without him. I could spend a whole day with these lads. They might even let me cut up a rabbit myself or even let me taste a cooked piece of one. In the end I give in.

'We have to go,' I say, and the two boys look at me surprised.

'We have to get back,' I say, and they seem to understand, but are sad about it and quiet.

'All right. See yez,' the older boy says and he steps away from us under the hedge along the side of the meadow, and his brother follows trailing one of the rabbits by its hind legs along the grass. We watch them for a minute before heading off ourselves in another direction, and Glancy says the word that turns everything that day all wrong and ugly, 'Tinkers,' and he gives a small laugh then, because he's seen how it shows on my face, what I am feeling inside, and I hate him that minute, every part of him and everything about him.

It is tea-time when we get back to the Barrack Field. Glancy says to me: 'We need to mobilise again tomorrow. The enemy is from the west. They have to go through the town. We'll ambush them when they do.'

'I'm not sure,' is all I can think of saying.

Like he sees all my secret thoughts on my face Glancy says then: 'We're warriors. We need to fight because that's what we are. That's what you're always saying to us.'

Glancy is like that: like a cat with something that he won't let go of. He has a war now of his own because he sees that I don't want it.

The next day in the Barrack Field he tells the gang that the enemy will soon come through the town and that they will have to be ambushed. He is all excited as he tells the other boys and I can see that he is challenging me because he looks at me all the time and then back to the others and then back to me again. He says that warriors need war because that's what warriors do, and anyone that does not want a war cannot be a warrior, the rules of the gang. He looks right at me and makes sure that everyone can see that he does.

I tell him that I am leader and that I do not want a war. This enemy is too strong for us, too many grown ups, and they have horses, dogs and caravans and we don't.

'You're out of the gang,' he says then in front of them all in a pleased tone of voice and smiling. 'You've broken the first rule of warriors.'

I can see how much he is enjoying it, being able to best me like this, and the red on my face that they all can see. Even the smaller ones in the gang are laughing at me now. I rush at him and we wrestle for a while on our feet and I have him grabbed around the waist trying to squeeze the life out of him and he has me by the neck. Stupid of me, the very thing I'd taught him ages before. He drops to the ground and bangs my head on it just like I'd shown him how, and I see stars and the fight goes out of me and he is standing over me, like a champion. The final bit to rub it all in, that he is in charge now: he helps me to my feet. He slaps me on the back then and tells me that I fought well and that he will be happy to keep me on as his second in command. I manage to smile at him, and he takes this for a yes, and they all cheer then for the new leader of the gang.

He has a war now and I just tag along all confused, not knowing where I should be, and I watch and wait, just like he did, except that I don't know why at this stage. He does all the preparations along the ambush position, getting the gang to put up strong-points on the end of the Barrack Field

127

wall that is over the street. He even finds out from one of the local guards that he is friendly with what day the enemy is being moved on. He makes the training even harder for the gang and I think that I don't care about any of it now, but I do in a way that I can't explain.

I tag along and, on the day, we are in position over the street with our cap guns and the enemy is advancing along: the horses pulling the caravans, the goats and dogs tied to the axles and the people walking alongside or behind. I am looking out for the two boys but I do not see them. They are probably in one of the caravans, and I am glad for that.

Then Glancy gives the order to fire and the whole gang starts shooting. I do not shoot. I am holding onto my cap gun, watching like someone looking at a horror film. The horses rear a small bit but not much. They are used to noise and children I suppose. The people do not look up at us. They look right ahead as they walk under the rapid fire of our cap guns. Then Glancy shouts 'Tinkers,' real loud and happy, like the word means Christmas or presents or something magic that we used to believe in when we were smaller, and one of the women puts her shawl back on her shoulders, looks up at us, and eyes me hard, like she recognises me, like I am the leader. She is a young mother, I am guessing. She has that look, and she is dark skinned and pretty like the heroines and queens that I see in our school books, and her eyes are flames of anger and pride. She throws her shoulders back then and walks on, probably knowing well that I will not forget this day or those eyes even if I live to be very old.

Lightning Source UK Ltd.
Milton Keynes UK
UKOW050609270312

189643UK00001B/3/P